Dana L. Harbour
from
Bill & Tom
Xmas, 1973

# HANNAH'S TOWN

## IN APPRECIATION

In presenting this captivating book about Pennsylvania's first County Seat west of the Alleghenies, The Westmoreland County Historical Society wishes to thank the following who made possible the wide distribution of HANNAH'S TOWN:

### Lions Club of Greensburg
*"Westmoreland County's Largest Service Club"*

### Pittsburgh National Bank

### Pepsi-Cola Bottling Corporation of Kecksburg

### Greensburg Saving and Loan Association
*"One Hundred Years of Service"*

### Westmoreland Casualty Company

### W H J B Radio Inc.
*"Westmoreland County's First Radio Station"*

Other Books
by
George Swetnam


Pittsylvania Country 1951

Bicentennial History of Pittsburgh 1955

So Stand Throughout the Years 1955

Where Else But Pittsburgh 1958

Star in the West 1958

Heroes of the Cross 1959
   published in the Pittsburgh *Catholic Journal*

The First 100 Years 1965

Pennsylvania Transportation 1964
   revised and enlarged 1968

*Contributor*

Presbyterian Valley 1958

# Hannah's Town

by

**Helen C. Smith**

and

**George Swetnam**

Illustrated
by
Helen C. Smith

Dillon/Liederbach Inc.

CLEVELAND

1973

HANNAH'S TOWN
by Helen C. Smith
and
George Swetnam

Published by
DILLON/LIEDERBACH, INC.
14591 Madison Avenue
Cleveland, Ohio 44107

*"Books should to one of these four ends conduce:*
*For wisdom, piety, delight or use."*

ACKNOWLEDGEMENTS

The Authors are deeply indebted to all those whose enthusiasm about Hanna's Town encouraged us in the writing of this book. We are especially grateful to those whose research in background material was made available. To the scores of dedicated volunteers who have literally dug up obscure and pertinent facts concerning the site.

To Jacob L. Grimm, curator at Ft. Legonier, Research Assistant at Carnegie Museum and Director of Archaeology; to Edward Smith, in charge of maps and surveys, and to his wife Mary Jane, who discovered the forget-me-not thimble; to Mrs. Margaret L. Fields, Mrs. Helen Wilson and her late husband, Kirke, whose knowledge of ceramics aided in identifying many artifacts unearthed at the site; to Charles Cunningham, Jr., co-ordinator of the dig; to Daniel J. Ackerman, who first told us about Hanna's Town; to Karl Koch, whose life long research of the folklore of the region gave us many insights about the life-style of the period; and to Peter Cholock, whose enthusiasm and devotion to the historic site is a continuing inspiration.

Members of the Westmoreland County Historical Society have been especially helpful, particularly Calvin E. Pollins, President of the Society; William Porter, Administrative Vice President; John A. Robertshaw, Jr., Treasurer, and Hazel Adams, Secretary to the President.

We also express appreciation to the Publishers, Dillon/Liederbach, Inc., for their helpfulness in making this book available.

# Contents

# i.

## *hooray for hanna's town*

"HANNAH! DO BE STILL," sighed Mother. "You're so impatient. Squirming around just like a wiggle worm."

Mother was busy trying to pin a new butter-nut yellow dress onto Hannah, with a cushion of straight pins in her hand. Mother spun the flax into thread, wove the linen, and sewed all the family's clothing.

"Oops, there goes another one," she said accidentally dropping a pin. "Aye, that's the second one that I've lost through the floor boards today. If I keep this up, I'll have to ask Father to make us some more." Mother began to sing to herself:

> See a pin and pick it up,
> and you'll always have good luck . . .

Hannah could hardly stand still any longer. She was

very anxious to get back to Jonathan. She was teaching her little brother his lessons.

Jonathan was playing on the floor with their dog while he waited. "Roll over, Shep," he said trying to teach his pet some tricks.

"There. Now you may run along, Hannah," said Mother at last. Hannah's chestnut-brown curls bounced up and down on her forehead as she skipped off to rejoin her brother.

"Now, Jonathan," said Hannah, "tell me again. What is your name?"

Her brother looked up and said, "My name's Jon'than."

"Jonathan what?"

"Jon'than West," was the reply.

How do you spell your name, Jonathan West?" echoed Hannah.

"J-O-," began her brother.

"J-O, jo; N-A, na," prompted Hannah.

"J-O-N-A," hesitated Jonathan.

"That's right. T-H-A-N, than," his sister said encouragingly.

Jonathan closed his eyes tight and tried once more. "J-O-A-"

"No, no," Hannah said. "JON—Oh well, for now just remember Jon. But some day, Jonathan, you'll be able to spell your whole name. You really will. Now we'll go on with the lesson. Where do you live?"

"In Hans'town," returned Jonathan.

"Where is Hanna's Town?" she asked. "What colony is it in?"

Jonathan always stumbled over the big word "Pennsylvania." But he finally managed to say something like it.

Before Hannah had a chance to ask another question,

Jonathan spoke up. He knew that his sister would ask him where Pennsylvania was. Jonathan quickly said, "In America."

"Good boy!" exclaimed Hannah. She clapped her hands and gave him a big hug. Jonathan was learning his lessons very well.

"I've taught him all of this," she thought with pride. "Maybe I have more patience than my mother thinks I have."

Hannah remembered being taught the same thing by her mother, for there were no schools where Hannah and her brother lived. Children were taught reading, writing, and ciphering at home by their parents or older brothers and sisters. Many never learned to read and write at all.

Ciphering still gave Hannah some trouble. She had learned how to count to a hundred and to do her sums, but taking away wasn't quite so easy.

After Jonathan had recited all his lessons for Hannah, he had become very quiet. Much too still for a little boy who was going on four years old. At last Jonathan said stubbornly: "It's not fair!"

"What's not fair?" asked his sister.

Without replying, Jonathan jumped up from the floor. He went over to the fireplace with their shepherd dog staying close at his heels. Mother had threaded a needle and was about to sew a bone button on Hannah's dress. Jonathan stamped his foot and repeated the same thing to his mother.

"It's not fair!" he protested.

Mother laid aside her sewing and looked at him with her warm blue eyes. She waited patiently for him to go on.

"If Hannah has a town, why can't I have one, too?" Jonathan asked very seriously.

Mother's puzzled frown turned into a smile.

"The town doesn't belong to Hannah," she explained. "It's just called that because it was started by Robert Hanna. You know where Mr. Hanna's house is," she went on. "There on the Great Road that General Forbes built. Mr. Hanna owned the land along the road. So he laid out streets and sold lots for people to build houses. It just happened that Hannah has nearly the same name as the town.

Hannah heard what her brother had said. "Come over here, Jonathan," she said. "Since your lessons were so good, I'll tell you a story."

She sat down on the cabin floor. When Jonathan had settled himself comfortably beside her, she began:

"When I was about the same age as you are now, we were living at Valley Forge—far, far away from here. One day Father and Mother decided that we ought to move west to find more land."

"Oh yes—how well I remember," interrupted Mother. "It was back in 1769, as soon as the Penn's would let anyone take up land here."

"And you weren't even born yet, Jonathan," added Hannah. "We loaded as much as we could into the wagon—our iron pot and skillet, an axe, a hoe, a sack of corn, and even Father's fiddle. He didn't think we should take the space for it, but Mother made him bring it along."

"The same horses that Father has now pulled us over the big, high mountains. And I remember Father walking behind the wagon with Shep."

"It took a whole month," reminded Mother.

"Yes, and for a while I thought it was such fun," went on Hannah. "I could ride in the wagon. There were good roads over the first mountains, and then there was a long way that was nearly level, and had lots of people living on farms. It took days and days, but sometimes the farmers would let us stop and rest, and even invite us into their houses to sleep."

Jonathan liked to hear his sister tell him stories and now he listened breathlessly to all that she was saying.

"Most of the time we camped out and spread our beds on the ground, close to the fire where Mother cooked. Sometimes when it rained we would sleep under the wagon, or take shelter under big trees."

"Then we came to the high mountains, where the roads went nearly straight up and down sometimes. And they were grown up with bushes, and there were big rocks and stumps. Going down the mountains Father would have to cut down a tree and tie a log on behind the wagon, to drag on the ground, so the wagon wouldn't roll against the horses and make them run away."

"Even I had to walk, until my feet got very sore from the hard stones in the road."

"Every time we came to a stream we had to ford it. Once the water was so deep that I could reach out and touch it as we crossed over."

"Were ya' ever scared?" asked Jonathan, with eyes open wide.

"Well, a little bit, sometimes in the big, dark forests that stretched for miles and miles. We could hear wolves howling and panthers screaming. And some nights we slept in the wagon because there were so many snakes. But it was nice, too, looking up at the stars through the openings in the trees—listening to the owls hooting."

"I wish I could have been there, Hannah," said Jonathan wistfully. "You have all the fun."

"Then we came to the Loyalhanna Creek," she went on.

"Is that your creek, too?" asked Jonathan before his sister had a chance to say anything more.

But Mother quickly came to her rescue. "No, honey," she laughed. "It's an Indian name. The 'Loyal' means middle and the 'hanna' is their word for water."

This seemed to satisfy Jonathan for the moment, so Hannah continued with her story.

"At last we came to a clearing one day, and there were cabins and people. Father and Mother liked this valley. There were many springs, and the soil was good. So this is where they wanted to settle. That was when I first saw Hanna's Town. And Father built our cabin right here at the bottom of this hillside."

All of a sudden Jonathan jumped up and trotted off with Shep, singing a little tune he had made up:

> Oh, your town, and my town, is Hanna's Town.
> Hooray for Hanna's Town
> Our town is Hanna's Town.

With Jonathan's song still ringing in her ears, Hannah watched the burning embers in the fireplace. She remembered that when she first heard the name Hanna's Town, she thought the village was her town, too, just like her brother. She was older now and knew better. But Hannah still secretly felt that it was her town. Her very own.

## ii.

# *hannah finds a friend*

THE JUNE SUN WAS just beginning to peek above the horizon. Out in the field the meadow larks were singing. Hannah could see rays of sunlight streaming between chinks in the cabin roof.

"Get up, Hannah," called Mother. "Make haste, if you want to go with Father to the house raisin'."

A new family had moved to Hanna's Town late in winter, and some of the neighbors were getting together to help them build their log cabin.

"I thought that was yesterday," said Hannah, rubbing the sleep out of her eyes.

"It takes three days to build a house," reminded Father, who had just come in from milking. "But I guess you were too young to remember how long it took to build ours.

"Yesterday we cut down the trees, trimmed all the logs,

and notched a few of 'em,'' he went on. "I didn't take you because it wouldn't have been anything very new. And besides, there's danger. When it's more than one man cutting more than one tree at a time, it's no fit place for children.''

"It's dangerous even for men. Jim Phillips came pretty near getting crushed yesterday when a fellow from over Loyalhanna way misjudged a tree. It twisted as it fell, and almost hit him.''

They had hoped Jonathan would sleep in that morning. But before breakfast was over he was awake and clamoring to go along, wherever Hannah was going.

"I don't think it would be safe for you," Mother said. "Someday when you're old enough, you may go to a raisin'. But not yet.''

Hannah rode sideways behind Father on Bob, who had been a wheelhorse in a freight team and was used to wearing a saddle. Bessie, their other horse, was young and sometimes got a little fractious if you tried to get her to carry double.

"I wonder," thought Hannah, "if it will be like the time when the neighbors got together to build our cabin.'' Thinking back, she was surprised by how much she could remember.

"Who taught you how to build a log house, Father?" asked Hannah.

"Oh, a long time ago I learned from my father, and grandfather taught him before that. And so,—on it goes. But if you go back far enough, I guess it was really those Swedes and Finns who started it all. This is one thing we settlers taught the Indians.''

It was about half a mile to the place, and back from the main road. Hannah slid off the horse and to the ground as they stopped. Father picked out a shady spot to tie old

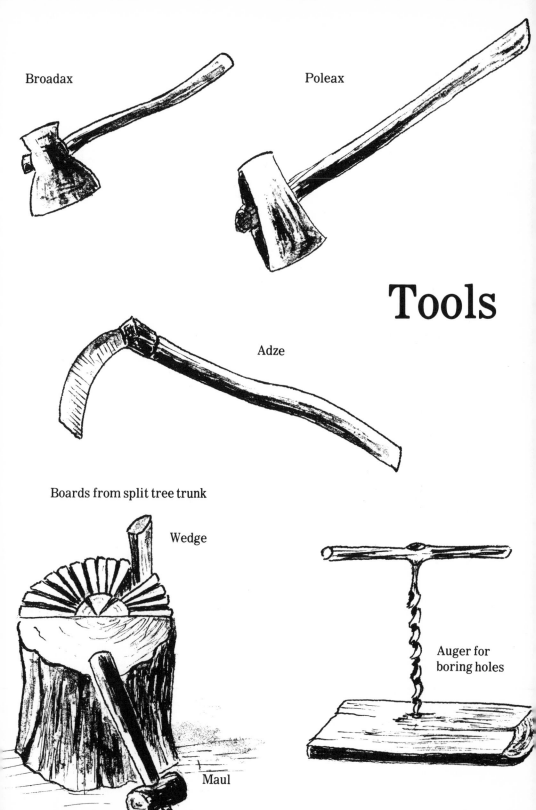

Broadax

Poleax

Tools

Adze

Boards from split tree trunk

Wedge

Maul

Auger for boring holes

Bob, and took his wooden maul and his sharp pole axe,
which he had carried in a sling for safety.

"A good axe is the best tool a man can have, even more
important than a rifle sometimes," he had often told her.
"But it can be the most dangerous, too."

There were already several men on hand, and she
wanted to hurry on, but Father stopped her.

"Be sure to stay far enough off that you don't get hurt or
get in the way," he warned.

The men were mostly talking about how to divide the
work. And since she couldn't hear much of what they
saying, Hannah looked around and spied some thick briers
in a clearing along the roadside. They were blackberries
and were getting ripe very early this year.

Hannah often picked berries with her mother, but they
were usually being saved for jam, jelly, or pies; and it was
a lot like work. "This time," she thought, "I'll get to eat
them all right from the bush and not have to save any."

They were luscious, but just as Hannah was reaching
out for the biggest one she could see, she stumbled over a
little stump.

"Oooow!" she cried—not very loudly—as she fell.

"Hello there," said a girl's voice. "Are you all right?"

Hannah picked herself up. Her arms and face were
scratched with the thorns of the blackberry bushes.

"Ye-es, I think so," she murmured, brushing herself
off. "Who are you?"

The girl standing before Hannah was about her own
height and had brown hair, too. Only it was straight and
hung in long, thick braids down her back.

"My name's Jennifer Bradford, but my folks call me
Jenny," she said as she helped pick out the thorns which
still stuck in Hannah's clothes and skin. "What's yours?"

"Hannah. Hannah West. I live down the road in Hanna's

Town. But it really isn't my town," she concluded with a smile. "Where do you live?"

"Right here," said Jennifer, pointing to where the men were getting the logs together and digging a square trench in the ground for the bottom ones. "This is our cabin that they're raisin' today. We've lived in our wagon ever since we started coming across the mountains. I can hardly wait 'till they build our house. Come on. Let's go over and watch."

The girls gathered up their linsey-woolsey skirts and ran over to a large tree. After straightening their bonnets, they settled down on the ground in full view of the place where the cabin was being built.

"I wonder how large your house is going to be?" asked Hannah. "Ours is great big," she bragged.

"I don't know," replied Jennifer. "But it's probably going to be larger than yours," she said in defense.

Hannah straightened her shoulders. "It will not," she snapped.

"It will so," retorted Jennifer, her eyes flashing.

"It will not!"

"It will so!" Back and forth, and on and on they argued. Hannah felt like slapping her new friend's face or at least pulling one of her braids. But Father was standing nearby, and she knew that he would be angry if she did. When each could see that the other one would not give in, they fell silent and began to watch the activity that was all around them.

Now the men who were most experienced with an axe stood at the four corners where the house was to be built. Hannah noticed with pride that her father was one of the corner men. The others were standing by the edge of the clearing. There was a great pile of logs that had been cut down the day before. They were hitching these, one at a time, behind a yoke of oxen. The big team then dragged the logs to where they were needed. The men often used their hickory handled axes as measuring sticks. One man measured the first log six axe handles and six hand breadths in length.

As the round, bark covered logs were brought to the site, the men at the corners notched them about a foot from the ends. They laid them in a square trench dug into the ground. The two longer sides were placed in position first, and then the two shorter sides were laid across the longer logs.

The notches held them in place. No nails were needed, but sometimes a man with a huge broadaxe and a sharp eye squared off rough spots, so that the logs would fit close together.

Now the logs looked like a large square frame on the ground with the ends extending out from the corners. The next layer was put in place in the same way. The men rolled each log up higher on two poles resting against the cabin sides. When a log was in place and ready to be raised, a man would call: "All together men, he-o, he! he-o, he!"

Hannah and Jennifer watched the cabin grow until it was nine logs high. "I wonder what they're going to build next?" asked Jennifer at last. Just then the girls heard the word "loft" mentioned by one of the men.

"Oh good," said Hannah. "It sounds like you're going to have a loft, too." By now the girls had forgotten their argument and were friends again.

"We never had one before," said Jennifer in wonder.

"Didn't you?" replied Hannah quite surprised. "Ours looks like a big wide shelf built right under the roof. It is over most of the cabin, but I can look down into the room below. I sleep in our loft at home. My father built a ladder out of boards, pegged to the cabin wall. That's for me to get up to it on.''

"Mother hangs some of the dried fruits and vegetables in our loft. You know, strings of red peppers, rings of pumpkins and all kinds of herbs in bundles. I like to lie awake at night and imagine what strange animals and things they look like, there in the dark shadows. Then I close my eyes and try to tell how many different smells I can recognize.''

For the loft, the men laid split logs across the short side of the cabin, so as to cover it all but about four feet at the end toward the road. With their split sides up, these made a sort of floor at the top of the ninth course of logs.

It was now well past noon. At last the men put down their axes and saws and wiped their foreheads. They stepped back for a better view. Father was the first to speak up:

"Well, it looks like your cabin's just about raised, Ben,'' he said turning to Mr. Bradford.

"Yes, Dan, and well done at that,'' replied the owner. "Now, let's get something to eat. Everyone must be as hungry as bears.''

Already Hannah could smell the sausage that Mother had sent along for the newcomers. Mrs. Bradford was frying it over an open fire. Several other women brought pot pies, fresh bread, pickled pig's feet, sliced bear meat, pretty relishes and pickles in stoneware crocks, and apple dumplings.

The men gathered over by the wagon, hungrily eating the food spread out on a split log. Hannah and Jennifer, quite good friends by now, ducked in among the neighbors and filled their wooden trenchers with food.

The men folk talked about the cabin and what further work had to be done, while the women got caught up on the latest gossip and exchanged recipes.

"The last apple pie I made tasted fine," one of the younger women said. "Only one thing though, Jake said a wagon wheel going over it wouldn't break the crust." The women all joined in merrily with laughter.

"Come on, Hannah, let's go over and see Billy and Bee," urged Jennifer between mouthfuls.

"Who're Billy and Bee?" echoed Hannah.

"They're my father's oxen," replied Jennifer. The big friendly red beasts stood patiently in the shade with the yoke still on their necks. They nodded their heads slowly as the girls patted them on the nose and flanks.

"Oh-h," squealed Hannah as one switched her with his tail, trying to brush the flies off his back.

"That's what our Bob does to me, too," she said. "Come with me and I'll introduce you to him." Hannah took Jennifer over to where her horse was standing. The girls led Bob off to the spring to give him some water.

On the way back, Hannah noticed some barrels over behind the Bradford wagon. "What's in those?" she asked curiously.

"That's how Ma brought our good pewter and blue and white dishes over the mountains from Philadelphia," explained Jennifer. "She's scared to unpack them for fear some of it might be broken."

When they returned, the men had finished eating. With much laughter and joking they went back to build the roof of the cabin. While the men worked, Hannah and Jennifer busied themselves making yellow daisy chains. They had to talk above the ringing of the axes and scraping of the saws and adzes.

The roof was built by cutting each successive end log shorter and shorter, and with the top notch almost half an axe-handle back from the one which rested on those at the sides.

This made it look something like a stair-step pyramid,

until the top notch on the shortest end log was right in the middle, with one log forming the comb of the roof.

The men with the axes had shaved off one side of each long log until they made more of a slanting line than stair steps.

"Are ya' ready for the clapboards yet?" called up one of the men to another on the roof.

"We've been ready for some time," he answered with a grin. "What took you so long?" he teased. The four-foot clapboards were laid on the roof. They looked like giant shingles overlapping one another. Then heavy weight poles were put across them and tied down with vines to hold the boards in place.

"We'll get the door cut out next thing," Hannah heard Father tell Mr. Bradford. "You can saw out your own windows at a time that suits you best. We lived in our house with no windows at all the first winter to save cutting so much firewood. Then the next spring I put in a window and hung skins in the opening. I built shutters for when the weather gets real bad. Later on we replaced the skins with paper, waterproofed with oil. The paper helps to keep out flies as well as the rain and snow."

"You'll want your door to open to the outside," one of the men advised Jennifer's father, "so that you can have more room inside. Believe me, you'll need all the space you can get."

The men quickly made a door by fastening boards together with pegs. They hung it onto the frame with wooden hinges which swung on pins. One of the neighbors carved out a wooden latch and attached a leather strap to it above a small opening that he bored into the door.

"When guests are welcome, you leave the latch string hanging on the outside," explained Hannah to Jennifer as she added another daisy to her long chain. "But at night, you can draw the strap inside, and no one can get in.'' They dodged as a big bumble-bee buzzed past them.

''I wonder if you're going to have a wooden floor,'' said Hannah curiously. ''We had a hard dirt floor at first and every time that it rained a lot, the water leaked through the roof and onto the ground. My mother had to spread straw over the mud so that we could walk.''

Hannah's question was soon answered. ''To make life a little easier for 'em, let's build a puncheon floor,'' suggested one of the men. ''It's not close dark yet, and we have enough split logs left over.''

''Fine idea,'' agreed one of the others. ''Let's get started. Times a'wastin.'' Several of the men quickly began smoothing them with adzes.

''What's a puncheon floor?'' asked Jennifer.

''It's a wooden floor made out of logs cut in half and laid very close together with their flat sides up,'' Hannah explained. She had watched her father split logs lengthwise with a maul and wedge and lay their floor about two years after they had moved in.

When the floor was laid, the chimney was built at one end of the cabin. The men first sawed out four short logs from one of the end walls.

''That looks like they're making another door,'' gasped Jennifer in surprise.

But just then the men put three short, smaller logs on the ground to form another square outside of the opening of the wall. More logs were placed on top of these in the same manner that the cabin was built until the chimney rose above the rooftop.

''That reminds me of a riddle,'' said Hannah.

''What's that?'' asked Jennifer.

''Patch upon patch and a hole in the middle, Tell me this riddle and I'll give you a fiddle,'' said Hannah.

Jennifer thought for a moment and then said, "I give up, what is it?"

"A chimney, of course," said Hannah.

"Oh, I knew all along," said Jennifer rather quickly. "I just didn't want to let on."

While the men were building the log chimney, the women and children helped press sticks, stones and moss in the cracks between the logs. Then they daubed clay in the chinks, and all over the inside of the chimney where the flames would be. This would almost bake into brick and keep the logs from catching on fire.

"Tomorrow we'll build the fireplace inside the cabin," Hannah overheard one of the men say as she daubed more clay in the gaps between the logs. She knew that the fireplace was a very special part of the log cabin, where all of the family's activities centered. Not only was it used the entire year round for cooking and for warmth, but it also provided most of the light in the cabin at night. And right over the fireplace Father always kept his rifle and powder horn handy.

"You know what, Hannah," Jennifer said as she stood back and looked at her new house. "Our cabin looks just like a big bird cage with all those spaces between the logs."

Hannah laughed, "It won't look that way tomorrow when they finish daubing moss and clay between the logs just like we're doing to the chimney."

Then it was Jennifer's turn to laugh, for Hannah had a big streak of clay mud across her nose and down over her cheek.

"Now that our cabin is almost finished, I wonder what we're going to sit upon and eat on," Jennifer remarked.

"Oh, just wait until tomorrow when they make your furniture," said Hannah. "They'll build a puncheon table and three-legged stools. And the men will peg some shelves to the walls to hold your mother's blue and white dishes."

"If they're not broken," reminded Jennifer.

"Then they'll probably build a bedstead into the wall for your mother and father to sleep on. And while they're doing all that, you know what we can do, Jenny," added Hannah.

"What?" asked Jennifer eagerly.

"We can make our own furniture."

Jennifer's eyebrows raised. "We can?" she said with surprise.

"Yes. I'll show you how to make doll chairs and tables by sticking together the prickly, brown cockle burrs that grow along the edge of the woods. Our dog Shep is always bringing some home, caught in his long hair."

By now it was nearing nightfall. The crickets could be heard chirping their evening song. As the crowd was breaking up to go home, Hannah thought of an idea.

"I know," she suddenly said to Jennifer. "Why don't you come home with us over night and you can sleep in our loft with me. Our house is so *big* and there will be plenty of room. I'm sure my folks won't mind. Then you can come back with my father in the morning when he returns to help finish the cabin. You can ride home with me on old Bob. He often carries both me and my brother on his back."

"I'll ask my ma," said Jennifer turning to see where her mother was.

"Are you sure there's room for Jenny?" asked Mrs. Bradford coming over to where Hannah and her father were standing.

"Old Bob would carry the whole family if need be," said Hannah's father as he smiled with great confidence in his horse.

Bob hardly noticed the extra load as Mr. Bradford

boosted Hannah and Jennifer up behind Father.

Benjamin Bradford took Daniel West's hand as he thanked him heartily for the help he had given him. "Couldn't have done it without you," he said.

"What good are we if we can't help one another," Father replied.

Father, the girls, and old Bob started down the dirt road toward Hanna's Town. After they had gone a short distance Hannah asked:

"Father, how big is our house?"

"Eighteen feet long and twelve feet wide," he replied. "The very same size as Jennifer's."

The girls glanced at each other and suddenly burst out laughing. Father had a puzzled look on his face, wondering what was so funny. They continued on their way; and the sun slowly disappeared from view, west of the newly raised cabin.

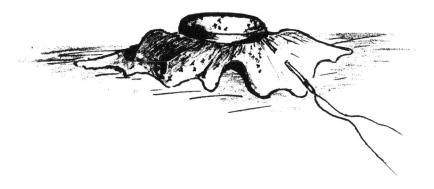

# iii.

## *the stranger*

IT WAS A SULTRY July afternoon in Hanna's Town. The sky was brilliant blue. There was not a cloud in sight. Along the edge of the woodlands Father was planting an apple orchard. Every so often he would stop and prop the spade up beside him as he wiped his brow. The flies continued to buzz in the sizzling sun.

"Hannah," called Mother from the cabin door. "Go to the spring and fetch me a bucket of water right away." Mother was bleaching linen white by wetting it down and letting it dry in the sun.

Sitting on a stump in the shade under the white oak tree that sheltered the cabin, Hannah was busy at her sewing. She had just run out of thread in her needle and was looking at her sampler. Mother sometimes called it an examplar, for Hannah had used different examples of stitches on the border and on the letters of the alphabet.

21

The sampler was very colorful. Mother had dyed the cotton threads into many pretty shades. From the sumac blossoms and poke berries she obtained crimson; yellow and orange from sassafras bark; rusty black from walnut hulls; and from butternut bark, brown and yellow.

But blue was very special. Mother had to trade her homespun linens and woolen goods for this color at the little shop in Robert Hanna's tavern or whenever a peddler came to town. It was expensive and hard to get, for it came from indigo, grown far away in the southern colonies.

And for green, her mother mixed indigo with goldenrod flowers and wood ashes.

Hannah had finished every letter of the alphabet except "Z", and was ready to cross-stitch it when Mother called her. She was glad, for by now her fingers were getting tired.

Quickly re-threading her needle, Hannah stuck it into her sampler and put the needlework in her apron pocket before starting for the spring.

As she passed the cabin door, she saw Jonathan playing on the floor with some clay marbles that Mother had baked for him. Hannah noticed a ray of sunshine falling on his light-colored hair. Father always called him a tow-head, for his hair was the shade of flaxen tow fibers.

"Jonathan," called Hannah. "Come with me to the spring house." Jonathan was eager to go with his sister. He jumped up and ran to Hannah. Shep followed close behind.

It was a pleasure on a hot day to make a trip to the cool, refreshing spring house. One of Hannah's regular duties was to get water for the family three or four times a day. It always felt good to splash the water on her hot face and arms. Sometimes it was so cold that it made her skin feel numb.

"Who made our spring house?" Jonathan asked as they set out for the little stone building beyond the foot of the hill.

"Father did," answered Hannah swinging the wooden bucket back and forth as she walked. "He built it soon after we moved to Hanna's Town. I guess you were too young to remember then."

"Why did he put it here?" Jonathan wanted to know.

"The ground was always damp at this spot and in the winter time ice formed. Father knew there must be a spring near by. He dug and dug, and sure enough, the water gushed out. So he walled in two spaces, one where we dip out water and then an overflow into the second, where Mother stores our milk, butter and cheese to keep them from spoiling.

"Then Father built the little stone house over it. And the water runs out of it into Crabtree Run below," Hannah said pointing to the streamlet of water.

"Can I dip the water out this time, Hannah? Please," begged Jonathan. He always liked to use the long, gourd dipper that Father had made. The narrow end of the gourd served as a handle. And the larger scooped-out end held the water.

Hannah pleasantly agreed. "Yes, Jonathan, this time it's your turn."

They had reached the spring house, but before opening the door, Hannah noticed something unusual. There were footprints in the soft ground below the building. She was used to seeing the tracks of deer, panthers, raccoons, bears, and foxes there. But she did not recognize these strange marks.

Suddenly Hannah heard a rustling noise in the bushes. A twig snapped on the ground. She looked up with a start. There beside the spring was a tall stranger from the woodlands. He had copper colored skin and long black hair. The man was wearing deerskin moccasins and a loin cloth. Three bright turkey feathers stuck up from his scalp lock. There were black and white shell beads around his neck. He carried a rifle and a knife hung from his waist.

Shep began to growl. The hair rose high on his neck.

Jonathan started to cry. He was afraid, for he had never seen anyone like this before. Jonathan hid behind Hannah's skirt and peeped around her at the stranger.

Hannah put her arm around him, trying to show more courage than she felt. She didn't want to frighten her brother by screaming.

"It's all right, Jonathan," she said in a consoling voice, to her own surprise.

Hannah knew that the stranger was an Indian. She thought of the stories she had heard about how hostile Indians scalped people. Even though she knew that he probably was friendly, she still had her doubts. "What if he isn't?" she thought with panic. Down deep inside, Hannah was frightened.

For a moment the girl stood speechless before the tall intruder. Then realizing how hot the day was, she suddenly thought of something. Disappearing into the spring house, she returned quickly with a dipper full of water. Jonathan followed his sister like a shadow. Hannah offered the water to the stranger. Immediately he took the gourd in both hands and after drinking until there was not a drop left, he bowed to show his gratitude. Then she pointed to the spring house and offered him some milk and cheese. But the Indian shook his head in reply.

Hannah had completely forgotten about her sampler,

which was hanging part way out of her pocket. Now for the first time she noticed the Indian eyeing it with admiration. He motioned to her that he wanted to see it. She tried to explain to him in English that it was not finished yet, but she was a little afraid not to give it to him.

"I still have some work to do on my sampler," hesitated Hannah uneasily. "See," she said shyly pointing to the last letter, "Y". "I have to stitch the 'Z' and then it will be finished." For a moment Hannah had forgotten that the Indian could not clearly understand all that she was saying.

The stranger paid no attention to what Hannah was trying to tell him, but kept admiring her work. She could see that she was getting nowhere with her explanation. "Oh, well," thought Hannah, "I might as well give it to him." "Here," she said as she presented her unfinished sampler.

The Indian was very much pleased, Hannah could tell. He pulled the needle out of the material and looked at it closely with satisfaction.

"He must be planning to take the needle, too," thought Hannah. "Maybe his squaw needs one."

She could see that he was waiting for something. Hannah knew how Indians liked to barter. So she timidly pointed to his collar of white shell beads and smiled. Father had told her one time that the Indians used shells for trading-money and called them wampumpeek, or wampum for short. The tribesman took the string of beads from around his neck and placed it around hers.

"Thank you," said Hannah politely. The stranger smiled. And with a bow and a flourish, he took his leave. The children watched him until he had disappeared into the thicket.

Then they raced back to the cabin as fast as they could go. Jonathan had a difficult time keeping up with his sister, for his short legs would not stretch as far as hers. But he was not far behind. They reached the door of the cabin, both out of breath and puffing.

"Mother, Mother!" cried Hannah. "We just saw an Indian, and I gave him a drink of water." Her eyes were wide with excitement.

"Did you offer him some food, too?" asked Mother. She knew that there were friendly Indians camped nearby on the Loyalhanna Creek, and she wanted to keep them that way. The Indians had been peaceful ever since Colonel Bouquet had quieted them with his army in 1764.

"I offered him some milk and cheese from our spring house but he didn't want any. Besides, he had a big piece of dried venison hanging in a pouch at his belt," replied Hannah.

"Yes," said Mother. "I understand. Indians never take more than they can use. Even when they are hunting wild animals, they will kill only what they need for food. They can't understand why white men are so wasteful."

Then Mother spied Hannah's collar of shell beads around her neck.

"Well, I declare—wherever did you get those?" she asked.

"The Indian gave them to me," answered Hannah proudly. "I traded my sampler for them."

"Were you finished with it?" asked Mother.

"No, but he didn't seem to mind."

"Very well, Hannah, but where is the pail of water?"

"Oh," cried Hannah remembering what she had set out for. "I guess I forgot. Come on, Jonathan. I'll race you back to the spring house."

"When you come back, I'll help you get started on another sampler," called Mother behind them. Hannah didn't mind having to make another one. She had traded her needlework for something she liked very much. And to Hannah, the Indian was no longer a stranger, but instead a friend. This she would always remember.

# iv.

# *from corn husks . . .*

IT WAS HARVEST TIME in Hanna's Town. The autumn sky
was as blue as the chicory blossoms that grew along the
roadside.

Wild grapes were getting ripe in the woods. They would
soon be gathered and dried into raisins to store for the
wintertime. Bright orange pumpkins, nubbly yellow
squashes, and long-necked gourds were lying in the
cornfields ready to be picked from their dry, withered
vines. Tall artichokes proudly displayed their yellow
sunflowers at the edge of the fields.

The wheat harvest was long past, and the grain had been
threshed out with flails. To Hannah it seemed like just a
short time ago that Father had made the journey with
their wheat to Denniston's grist mill. The summer had
gone quickly. And now it was time to cut the corn and get it
ready for another trip to the mill on the Loyalhanna
Creek.

27

Yesterday Father and Hannah had spent the day cutting stalks and leaning them together into shocks. Then they husked several bushels right there in the field.

Nothing was wasted. The corn would be ground into meal and used for bread and mush. They would pull the fodder, and the husks would be fed to the cow and horses. Father would save the stalks for bedding in the stalls.

The rough husks had scratched Hannah's fingers. Father had noticed it and said, "I'd better make you a husking pin." He took out his knife and whittled a wooden peg. Then he found a piece of leather and put a strap on it to fit onto her hand. The peg caught the loose ends of the husks and they slipped down off the ears much more easily.

In the evening hours after supper, the family sat before the fire shelling the dry corn that Father and Hannah had gathered. Every so often Father threw in some corn cobs to keep the fire burning brightly. A few he gave Shep to chew.

Hannah could see the harvest moon rising above the oak tree through the open cabin door. In the warm, autumn evening it looked like a big, ripe pumpkin shining in the sky. "What a pretty night," thought Hannah.

Jonathan noticed it too. "Why is the moon orange?" he asked.

"It's always that color just after the equinox. And it stays round for several nights instead of just one as usual. The next full moon will be the hunter's moon," said Father.

"What's a—a eekanox?" asked Jonathan, stumbling over the new word.

"That's the time when the center of the sun crosses the equator and the day will be as long as the night," said Hannah importantly. "This happens twice a year. Once in the fall and once in the spring.'' Father had explained all this to her the day before.

Jonathan looked in wonder at the moon. "It's almost as big as a wagon wheel," he said.

Now Hannah watched as Father shelled kernels from the ears by twisting his hands around the corn. Her hands were not big like Father's so he showed her how to take the corn off by running her thumb along the ear, taking one or two rows off at a time. After that, it was easy to twist the other rows off into the vacant spaces.

While Hannah rowed the corn with her thumb, Mother scraped her ears of corn over a frying pan to get the kernels off. Each had a different way of doing it. Jonathan watched everyone with curiosity.

As they worked, Father looked very thoughtful. "Hannah," he asked, "did you ever notice that there's always an even number of rows on an ear of Indian corn'?"

"What's an even number?" asked Jonathan as Hannah began to count the rows of corn on the ear in her hand.

Looking up, Hannah explained to her brother, "You know how to count up to ten. Well, skipping every other number and counting by two's you would say 2, 4, 6, 8 and 10. The other ones - 1, 3, 5, 7 and 9 - are called odd numbers."

But by now Jonathan had lost interest, yawned, and started to roll on the floor with Shep.

Hannah had counted eight rows on her ear of corn. The next one had ten. Some ears even had twelve. But the number was always even, just as Father had said.

Hannah looked up in amazement. "Why aren't there any with an odd number of rows?" she asked her father.

"I don't know, Hannah, but someday someone may discover the reason."

"Maybe the Indians could tell us," suggested Hannah. "We got Indian corn from them, didn't we?"

"Yes, we did," said Father. "But I doubt if they would know, either. They did show us many ways to use it, though. They have helped us, and we have taught them things, too . . not all of it good, I fear."

"We use their method of clearing the land, by girding a ring of bark all around the trees. When the circle of bark is taken away the tree dies, and the leaves fall off letting the sunshine through to the crops. But we chop up the dead trees for firewood instead of burning them down, as they do.

"The Indians taught us how to plant the corn in hills, five seeds to each mound:

> One for the blackbird,
> One for the crow,
> One for the cutworm,
> And two to grow.

"They were the first to plant pumpkins, squashes, and beans in corn fields. You know we plant beans after the corn is a few inches high and then the stalks later serve as bean poles for the vines to climb on."

"That's a good idea," declared Hannah. "Bean poles that grow!"

"The Indians have many good ideas, Hannah," said Father. "After all, they were living on the land before us and they know it well.

"They not only planted the different kinds of corn—field corn, sweet corn, and of course pop corn—but they know how to preserve it, too.

"Sometimes they dig a hole in the ground and put the

unhusked ears in it, covering them with grass and soil.

"Another way is to char it. They pick the corn before it is ripe. Then they roast the ears in hot ashes and shell the kernels off to dry in the sun. Maple syrup is added to the meal. The women make this "nocake" as it is called, for them to take on long trips. They add water or snow to it when they're ready to eat it. The corn will keep for years when it is prepared like this."

"Do the Indians take their corn to the grist mill like we do, Father?" asked Hannah.

"No. They usually use a mortar and pestle to grind their grain. The mortar is made out of a big block of wood. They burn a hole about a foot deep into the wood. Then they put the grain into it and use a rounded stone to crush the corn into meal. And if we didn't have a grist mill near by, that's the way we would have to do it, too."

"What else do they make out of their corn?" asked Hannah.

"Well, first of all they save the largest and best ears of corn and dry them, hanging the ears by their husks, for seed. We do this too, for if we didn't we wouldn't have anything to plant for next year.

"They make meal for bread and mush, just as Mother does. Then some of the grain they soak in lye, made by letting water run through wood ashes. That loosens the hulls, and when they wash it they get hominy.

"And of course they make succotash by cooking corn and beans together. But instead of mixing pork fat with it, as we do, they use dog meat. Only for ceremonial meals or to honor an important visitor, though."

Hannah's eyes widened as she clapped both of her hands over her mouth in surprise. She glanced over at Shep lying peacefully beside the fire.

"Don't worry, Hannah," chuckled Father. "We'll always have a good supply of pork from the hogs out in the woods. And if we don't, we'll go a-huntin'."

They fell silent for a few minutes, working steadily along.

"Here's a red ear," Father said suddenly, holding it up. Some of the corn was white with blue, brown or yellow kernels mixed together. But this ear happened to be all red.

Quick as a wink Father leaned over and kissed Mother. "According to the laws of husking," he said with a grin, "for each red ear that you find, it brings you luck, and you get to kiss your sweetheart." Mother's face blushed to a rosy pink. Father's blue-gray eyes twinkled as he winked at her.

Then he went on with his stories and told the children how the earlier settlers had bought the land from the Indians. "In fact, the proprietors wouldn't allow us to buy any farms west of the mountains until they agreed to it in a treaty in 1768 at Fort Stanwix, four years ago."

"Way up in New York?" Hannah asked.

"Yes," said Father. "The Quaker, William Penn was a friend to the Indians. He was a good man—and a fair man—he tried to keep peace with 'em at all times. He thought he'd try what love would do."

"By the way, Hannah, his wife's name was the same as yours. Hannah Penn managed all the colony after her husband died and later her sons took over for her."

Hannah's face beamed with delight. It seemed to her that Father always had some interesting story to tell.

By now Jonathan could hardly keep his eyes open, and Hannah was getting tired, too. She yawned and stretched her arms into the air.

"Well, I guess it is time for some children to be off for

bed," said Mother. That was always a signal for Father to bring out the big Bible from the shelf along the cabin wall.

He began to read to the family from Psalm 128:

> Blessed is every one that feareth the Lord;
> that walketh in his ways.
> For thou shalt eat the labour of thine hands;
> happy shalt thou be,
> and it shall be well with thee.
> Thy wife shall be as a fruitful vine
> by the sides of thine house;
> thy children like olive plants round about thy table.

When he had finished reading, Mother kissed Hannah and Jonathan good night. As Hannah climbed to her bed in the loft, she could hardly wait for morning to come, for tomorrow she was going with Father to take the corn to the grist mill. "I wonder if Jenny will be there," she thought to herself.

In another moment she was fast asleep.

# V.

# *. . . to hominy*

THE SUN FINALLY ROSE, and Hannah dressed as fast as she could. Mother had some hominy and a noggin of fresh milk waiting for her by the time she got down from the loft.

Wooden Noggin

"Here's some johnny cake to take along with you," Mother said as she placed a basket on the table.

"Why is that called johnny cake?" asked Hannah picking up her pewter spoon.

"Land sakes, child," said Mother, yawning sleepily. "You're so full of questions, even at this time in the morning. Johnny cake is just another name for journey cake. Since Jonathan could never say the 'r' we just got used to calling it johnny cake, for him. And you better hasten and eat, or you won't be going on any journey with your father to the mill—johnny cake or no johnny cake. You know how he doesn't like to wait."

Hannah quickly put on her freshly ironed bonnet and skipped out the door. Father was already loading the heavy bags of corn onto the wagon. The horses were hitched, stamping their feet now and then, anxious to be on their way.

Mother waved to them from the cabin door. "Don't forget to pick up Bradford's corn," she reminded. It was Father's turn to take the neighbor's grain to the mill along with his own.

"Oh, Father, can Jenny go with us?" asked Hannah turning eagerly to him.

"I reckon so," he said, snapping the reins for the horses to start. Bob and Bessie looked shiny and sleek with their long black tails and manes. Father let Hannah take the reins until they got to the Bradford farm.

When they arrived at the new log cabin, Hannah could see Jennifer waiting with her father by the roadside.

Father helped Hannah bring the horses to a halt. "How about letting Jennifer go along with us, Ben," he suggested.

"Certainly, Dan," Mr. Bradford said as he loaded his grain onto the wagon. And then lowering his voice Hannah over-heard him say, "I would have had a mighty disappointed girl here, if you hadn't asked.

"See you when you get back," he called, helping Jennifer up on the seat beside Hannah. "Hope the rain holds up."

Hannah had not seen her friend since the night that they stayed together in the loft after the cabin raising.

"How far is it to the mill, Mr. West?" asked Jennifer excitedly after they had gone a short distance.

"Well, I really can't say, Jenny," Father admitted, "but there's one way to find out." With this, he stopped the horses, reached into his pocket and took out a piece of twine. He tied it to one of the spokes of the right, front wagon wheel. Father gave Hannah a stick and his jack knife.

"I've been wanting to know this myself," he murmured.

"Now, Hannah, you and Jenny notch the stick every time that the wagon wheel makes a hundred complete turns. When we get there we'll be able to add up the marks and tell how many miles it is to the mill."

The girls began to keep track of every time the string came up to the top of the wagon wheel. "One, two . . ," began Hannah. The horses started off at a trot, and for a few minutes it was all the girls could do to count.

This kept them busy and the time seemed to go fast. In about two hours they came in sight of the log mill. The girls had counted thirty notches and eighteen turns. The wheel had turned 3,018 times.

"Let's see," said Father, "that wheel is about four feet across, which makes it close to twelve and a half feet around. Now, let's find out how well you can cipher." He looked on the ground until he found a piece of charcoal.

Writing on the side of the wagon, Father helped the girls figure a few minutes. "It's 37,725 feet," said Hannah looking at the numbers.

"That's right," replied Father. "There are 5,280 feet in

an English mile. Now we'll divide the number of feet
we've come by that figure." Father worked it out on the
wagon for them. "It's seven miles, with 765 feet left
over," he said at last. "Now, a furlong is an eighth of a
mile, or 660 feet. Allowing for not being exact on the size of
the wheel, let's say that we've come seven miles and one
furlong or a little more."

"That's a lot of ciphering," said Hannah taking a deep
breath.

"Well, at least we know how many miles it is to the mill,
now," replied Father.

"Let's keep count again on the way home and see if it
comes to the same number of turns," suggested Jennifer.
She had to speak up, for by now they could hear a roaring
noise as the water bubbled and splashed over the giant
wheel that turned the millstones inside the building.

It was Jennifer's first trip to the mill, and she gazed
wide-eyed at the big moss-covered water wheel turning
slowly. They watched the men raising sacks of grain to the
top story with a rope and pulley. Even the rattle of the
corn coming down the chute and the grinding of the
millstones fascinated them.

The girls jumped down from the wagon. Some of the
other farmers were already there and waiting in line to
take their turn at the mill.

Father went over to join the men. They were discussing
crops, weather and latest happenings. The girls listened
for a while to the conversation.

"I saw Reverend McClure the other day," one of them
said. Hannah knew that the man he mentioned was the
Presbyterian circuit preacher. He came through the area
from time to time to baptize little children, join couples in
marriage, conduct funerals, and preach sermons.

"Yes," the man went on, "and I understand he was

through last month, too. Stopped at Colonel Proctor's on his way and preached some. Chief Guyasuta was there. The Indian listened to his sermon as sober as a judge."

Hannah remembered the Indian at the spring house late in the summer. "I wonder if he could have been one of his braves," she thought.

Then the conversation changed. They were discussing land problems. "Right now I don't know for sure whether my farm is in Virginia or in Pennsylvania," a man in buckskin said. "Since Lord Dunmore is claiming it for Virginia and of course the Penns say it is part of their grant, how are we to know where we stand?"

"I don't know," said another. "But I made my claim with Virginia because they charge less for an acre of land."

Hannah and Jennifer were getting tired of the grown-up talk by now and ran over to a large oak tree.

"Have ya' ever made a corn husk doll, Hannah?" asked Jennifer as she reached down and picked up a big shiny, brown acorn.

"No," replied Hannah. "Let's make one."

There was a corn field nearby, and the girls returned shortly with some dried husks, bleached ivory white in the sun.

"First you start with an acorn," said Jennifer as she held one out in her hand. She removed the cup with her thumb.

"Then you soak the husks in water to make them soft," she went on. It didn't take Hannah long to run over to the creek to dampen them. When she returned, Jennifer wrapped one of the husks around the acorn and tied it with a narrow piece of the same material. Then she continued to make the arms and dress.

When that much was finished, the girls put some dried

# CORN HUSK DOLL

**1.**

Remove cup
from acorn.

Dampen corn
husks in
water.

**2.**

Wrap a husk
around acorn
and tie with
a narrow
strand of
husk for
the neck.

**3.**

Twist one
narrow husk and
tie at both ends for arms. (4 inches long)

**4.**

Tie the ends of
10 husks in place
around neck.

Bend arm piece
and place between
the 10 husks—
5 husks on one
side of arms
and 5 on the other.

**5.**

Tie all 10
husks together
around waist.

**6.**

Trim husks off around neck.

Trim bottom of skirt even to make dress 5 inches long.

**7.**

Place 2 narrow husks across each shoulder.

Criss-cross at waist.

Tie in place.

**8.**

Add dried corn silk for hair.

Tie a corn husk around head for a bonnet.

Paint a face on doll.

**9.  BROOM**

Twist one narrow husk and tie at both ends for handle. (6 inches long)

Gather 2 short husks around bottom of handle, 2 inches from end.

Tie and trim.

Shred broom husks with needle.

corn silk on the doll's head for hair. They tied a small strip of the husk around the head for a bonnet.

"And now for the face," Jennifer said. She found some poke berries still hanging on a stalk nearby and squeezed them out onto a rock. With the end of a twig for a brush, she used the red juice to make the eyes, nose, and mouth. Then they made a broom for the doll with a few short corn husks.

"How pretty!" exclaimed Hannah when they had finished.

"Here, Hannah, you may have it. I have another one at home," said Jennifer, handing the new doll to her friend.

"Oh, thank you, Jennifer," said Hannah.

Just then Father called the girls. "It's time for our corn to be ground now."

"Good," exclaimed Hannah jumping up with the new doll in her hand. "Can we watch?"

"Come along," said Father. "But be very careful your skirts don't get caught in the machinery."

Their corn had already been hoisted to the upper story of the mill. The girls followed Father up on an open-sided stairway and gazed in wonder at the wooden shafts and cog-wheels and caught glimpses of the big millstones whirling around.

On the second floor they met the miller, whose hat and clothes were white with dust from grinding corn and wheat. As he emptied the bags, he measured the grain carefully before putting it in the tub-shaped hopper.

Watching the process, Hannah suddenly grew suspicious.

"Father!" she whispered. "He's putting some of our corn in that bin, instead of into the hopper!"

Father laughed. "That's the way he gets paid for grinding our corn, Hannah," he explained. "The miller gets one-eighth of the grain. That's half a peck from each bushel. He can use it or sell it.''

After seeing the level of the corn in the hopper begin to sink, they went downstairs where a helper was catching the meal in the owner's bags as it came out of a wooden spout from the stones.

As fast as one bag was filled he slipped it aside and hung another in its place, hardly losing a handful in the process. Then he whipped a cord around the bag mouth, tied it, and cut it off, all in one motion.

Suddenly he heard a whistle from the miller and dropped a paddle into the chute, cutting off the flow of meal.

''That's where our meal begins,'' said Father. Sure enough, the man moved over a half-empty bag, tied it, and put one of theirs in its place. Then he pulled up the paddle and let the meal flow.

The helper smiled as he saw how intently the girls were watching.

''Would you like to taste it?'' he asked, catching a little in his hand as it fell into the bag and put it in his mouth.

Hannah held out her hand. ''It's warm!'' she said as she touched it. ''And it tastes so good.''

''That's from the heat of the millstones rubbing against one another,'' Father explained.

When their corn had been ground and the bags tied, Hannah counted them. ''Why, there's as much as there was before the miller took his toll,'' she gasped.

''That's right,'' Father told her. ''Grinding loosens up the grain, to where seven parts take as much space as eight parts of corn. Maybe that's how it came about that the toll was set at one-eighth.''

When Father had brought the wagon around to a little platform at the mill door, they loaded the bags.

"Now, Mother will have plenty of Indian meal for a while," he said.

It was time to make the long journey back home. Dark clouds were beginning to form in the sky. "We better hasten before we get drenched," urged Father.

Soon they came to a bend in the road. There was a whirring noise. Ahead of them a ruffed grouse flapped its wings hurrying to get out of the way.

Darkness was beginning to descend around them now. The woods on both sides of the road were so dense with trees that hardly a ray of light shone through.

Finally they could see the new cabin in the distance. Father dropped Jennifer and her sacks of corn meal off. They said goodbye to the Bradfords and started on the last half mile home.

There was a hint of rain in the air. Father held his hand up and felt a few drops. It was a good thing that they would be home shortly.

"We forgot to count the wagon wheel turns on the way back," Father said to Hannah. But it was just as well, for Hannah had snuggled up next to her father and was fast asleep. He put his arm around her to keep her from falling. And Hannah still held on to her corn husk doll. It had been a long day.

# vi.

## *county chair? county seat*

Hannah and Jennifer were perched on the stake-and-rider fence outside the door of the West cabin. It was a crisp, windy day in the month of March. A strong gust of wind almost blew the girls' sun-bonnets off. They were working on their hand looms, making yarn braids to hold their hair back.

Hannah had only seen Jennifer once since the day they went to the mill together. Mr. Bradford had brought Jennifer with him when he came to see Hannah's father about getting some seed potatoes for spring planting.

"Oh, Jenny," cried Hannah after the grown-ups had gone inside, "how I wish that you had been in our loft the other night with me."

"Why?" asked Jennifer curiously.

"I had gone sound asleep," continued Hannah, "when I was waked by the sound of voices. There were a lot of men sitting around the fire talking with Father and smoking their clay pipes. It had to be something very important because there were candles burning." Jennifer knew that candles were tiresome to make and tallow was scarce.

Hannah excitedly told her friend what she had heard.

"The men were talking about the new county that was formed last month. And it's going to be called Westmoreland, named after one by the same name in England. There was an Englishman who said it like WEST-more-LAND, but Father and all the others said it like West-MORE-land.

"Isn't that a perfect name!" Hannah went on. "For all of us came west to get more land."

"Yes," agreed Jennifer. "And Hannah West came west to Westmoreland." Both girls giggled until they almost fell off the fence.

"The county will be as big as the whole province this side of the top of the mountains," said Hannah. Nobody knows yet how much is in Pennsylvania or Virginia. Anyway, it takes in Fort Pitt.

"People in Westmoreland County will get to elect a member of the Pennsylvania Assembly, a sheriff, and other officers," Hannah said with importance. "There will be just one place for everybody to vote. And you'd never guess where that will be."

"Here?" Jennifer gasped. "Could it be here?"

"Right in Hanna's Town, Jenny. At Robert Hanna's tavern. Isn't that exciting?"

"What will they do besides vote?" asked Jennifer.

"They'll have courts," answered Hannah. "My father said this was very important, because these would be the first English courts ever held on this side of the mountains.

"The Pennsylvania Assembly named twenty-six men to act as justices in their own neighborhoods. And one of ours will be Mr. Hanna.

"Will the courts be here, too?" asked Jennifer.

"The courts will meet at the tavern for a while," said Hannah. "That's until they build a courthouse. And all of them hope it will be at Hanna's Town, too."

"How will they decide?" asked Jennifer curiously.

"I'm not sure," Hannah admitted. "One of the men said that some justice named Mackay thought it ought to be at Pittsburgh, because there are more people living around Fort Pitt. They said he didn't think there were enough tables and chairs at Hanna's for the men to sit in and write on. Nor room enough for all the people. He was afraid they would have to hold the courts outside under a tree with their papers all getting wet if it rained. That was why he didn't think Hanna's Town ought to be the county seat."

Just then Jennifer began to laugh.

"What's so funny?" demanded Hannah.

"I was just thinking they ought to call Hanna's tavern the county seat because there is just one chair there, and the whole county would have to sit on it."

"Then it better be a mighty big chair," snickered Hannah.

When both of them had stopped laughing, Hannah told Jennifer that just before she had gone back to sleep, the men were talking about how they would have to build a jail and a pillory and a whipping post at the county seat.

"Then I hope it won't come here," said Jennifer, her eyes as round as saucers. "I don't think it would be very nice to see people in jail, or with their head and hands locked in a pillory. And I wouldn't want to watch people being whipped on their bare backs until the blood runs down."

"No," agreed Hannah in a serious tone. "And especially not so close to home. If it has to be done, I'd rather it would be somewhere else. County seat or no county seat."

Hanna's Town Courthouse, Jail and Pillory

1773

# vii.

## *eavesdropping*

HANNAH AND JENNIFER HAD never seen so many people in town, they agreed. The girls had just met at the blacksmith shop where Father and Mr. Bradford had come to have their horses shod.

"Not even half so many," said Jennifer. "Where could they all have come from?"

"From all over the new county," said her father. "From Redstone, Georges Creek, Yough'ogheny, the Catfish settlement and all around. This is court day.

"And I hope you will both always remember this day," said Father. "This is a very important one. Today, April 6, 1773 is the first time an English court has ever been held west of the great mountains.

"And to make sure you don't forget, I'm going to give you something to remember it by," he went on, giving each one a playful box on the ear. Jennifer squealed with

51

surprise, but Hannah was ready. She remembered Father
telling her how his grandfather had once boxed his ears
very hard so that he wouldn't forget seeing a basilisk in a
fire.

"The old folks thought it was proof against fire," Father
had told her. "But the basilisk was only a lizard brought in
with the wood. Grandfather took a stick and flipped it
back into the fire to see the miracle. But he was sorry
afterwards, because it burnt up, poor thing."

Almost across from the blacksmith shop was Hanna's
tavern, turned for the day into a courthouse. It was
crowded with men dressed in every possible way. Some
had on knee-breeches, stockings, coats, and ruffled
sleeves and collars. Others were wearing homespun
clothes, and many had on long hunting-shirts of deerskin.
Because it was chilly, some of them wore caps made from
the skins of raccoons, opossums, or bobcats. A few of the
most important looking ones wore tall beaver hats.

"You can tell the coonskins by the striped tails they
always leave on'em," Hannah explained. "The 'possums
have that gray, silky hair, and the spotted ones are bobcat.
That brownish gray one is from a fox."

"Aren't you afraid of all those strangers?" asked
Jennifer.

"I would be," said Hannah, "but Father says that now
we'll have law and order in the name of King George III."

Some men came out of the tavern and others
boisterously pushed their way in. There was much merry-
making; everyone seemed to be having an uproariously
good time.

"Come on, Jenny," urged Hannah. "Let's run over and
see if we can find out what's going on."

Men were crowded around the open door and others
peered in the low window at one side. The girls slipped
around to the back and found a crack where the space

between the logs hadn't been very well chinked, and they could get a glimpse inside.

"See the tall man dressed so fine?" Hannah pointed out to her friend. "That one must be Colonel St. Clair. I think the one in the middle is Colonel Crawford. Look, there's Mr. Hanna, too, with his back towards us."

"I still can't see the big county seat," giggled Jennifer. The girls looked at one another and burst out laughing.

In front of the room some men sat on rough hickory chairs on a clapboard platform.

Everyone inside seemed to be talking at once. Then Justice Crawford rapped a carpenter's mallet on the table in front of him, and began to speak. All became quiet. Even Hannah and Jennifer stopped their whispering.

For a while various men talked, but it was hard to be sure what it was all about. Then the justice rapped for order again, and a clerk stood up and began to read. It was something about dividing the county into eleven townships. His voice droned on, naming them and giving long descriptions: "Fairfield, beginning at . ." And they finally made out: "to run down the Loyal Hannon to Chestnut Ridge . ."

Next came "Donegal." "You'd know that, with so many Scotch-Irish living around here," whispered Robert Hanna, loud enough for the girls to hear.

Then came Huntingdon, Mount Pleasant, Hempfield. "Beginning at the mouth of Crabtree Run, and running down the Loyal Hannon to the junction of the Conemaugh . ." The voice trailed off, and the next they heard was ". . up Jacob's Creek to the line of Mount Pleasant."

"That's us, Jenny," Hannah almost squealed and quickly put her hand over her mouth. Then came the other townships: Pitt, Tyrone, Springhill, Menallen, Rostraver, and Armstrong.

Suddenly one of the men inside heard their whispers and saw them peeking through the chink. The scowl on his face made the girls giggle. But just for a moment, for others were looking, too. With red faces Hannah and Jennifer ran back to the blacksmith shop and their fathers.

"We're living in Hempfield Township," Hannah announced importantly. "We listened at a crack behind the tavern and heard all about it."

"We could have told you that, already," said Father severely. "We both and nearly everyone else signed a petition for it. And by the way, it isn't nice to eavesdrop."

"There's something else you might think about," he went on, pointing to where some men were using heavy logs to build a small, one-room cabin without any window or chimney.

"What is it?" they asked together.

"That," said Father winking at Mr. Bradford, "is a jail, and people who are accused of doing something wrong may be kept there for months at a time waiting to be tried."

"Yes, sir," Hannah said softly.

Both girls hung their heads as they walked away a few steps.

"I don't think I'll ever eavesdrop again," Hannah told Jennifer soberly.

# viii.

## *spring greens*

"HANNAH," ASKED MOTHER. "WHY aren't you eating your supper? Aren't you feelin' well?"

Hannah looked up from her porringer of corn-meal mush with a start. She shook her head. Hannah had been day dreaming and dawdling with her food.

Porringer

"Oh, I guess I'm not very hungry," she stammered. Hannah was tired of eating dried foods and salted meats. She didn't want to hurt her mother's feelings. She knew

55

that there were no fresh greens or fruits to be had at this time of the year. Even the sauerkraut and pickled beans were all gone. It was always this way near the end of the winter.

Mother seemed to sense Hannah's feelings. "Spring will soon be here, and we'll be able to go into the woods and gather all kinds of fresh plants," said Mother reassuringly. Hannah felt much better and finished her meal quickly now.

At last spring did come to Hanna's Town. Tiny green shoots began to push their way up through the final snow of the winter. The sun melted away the last patch of frozen white from the north hillside overlooking the hamlet.

Pink and white buds on the crabapple and dogwood trees were starting to come out. Mother's lavender lilacs by the doorway perfumed the air with the scent of their blossoms.

Every day Hannah watched the new growth appear along the edge of the woodland. Mother's mint that she had brought from the East was already beginning to sprout.

"I'm going to fetch some greens in the woods, Hannah," said Mother one day. "Want to come along with me?"

"Oh, yes," answered Hannah eagerly. She was hungrier than ever for something fresh.

"Jonathan," said Mother, "you stay here with Father until we come back. He'll be needin' you to round up the hogs."

Mother and Hannah took a basket and started out for the woods behind their cabin. It was morning and the dew still sparkled on the grass. They walked along a narrow path which followed an Indian trail where buffalo had once roamed.

There were peeling sycamores, or buttonwood trees, as Mother called them, growing among the oaks and maples. Soft moss and feathery, green ferns grew on top of fallen trees.

Between broken branches and stumps, the black, rich earth from decaying leaves could be seen. Here and there along the path, Indian pinks and wild lavender phlox had poked their heads up looking for a place in the sun. Overhead the woodpeckers and wild pigeons fluttered and squawked a complaint at the intrusion of their privacy.

Everywhere Hannah looked the woods were dark, damp, and mysterious. The very tips of the giant oak trees seemed far, far away and ever so small compared to their big thick trunks. There was very little sky showing through the leaves. Some trees were so close together that they almost seemed to touch.

"Watch your step, Hannah," cautioned Mother. But no sooner had she warned her than Hannah tripped over a small sapling while looking up into the tree tops above her head.

Now Hannah was painfully aware of the young tree at her feet. Mother helped her up and brushed her off. "I'm all right," she said, soon forgetting her fall. Looking more closely at the sapling she had stumbled over, Hannah said: "That looks like sassafras." She knew that Mother used the roots and bark to make tea in the spring time for a tonic.

"We won't bother to take any now, Hannah. There's plenty around the cabin. The more we dig up, the more they seem to sprout.

"But look at the leaves, Hannah," Mother went on. "There's three different kinds; single bladed, mitten shaped, and three-lobed."

Hannah found a leaf having each shape. "And they're all growing on the same branch," she exclaimed with delight.

Now they were walking through an evergreen thicket. The dried needles made a soft path and the scent of pine was everywhere.

At last they came to a clearing. At the edge of the woods Mother spied some wild onions. "These will be good with our venison and dumplings tonight," she said as she placed them in her basket. Now the only thing that Hannah could smell was onion.

The trees along the edge of the meadow were a golden green in the sunlight. In some places the grass growing at the base of their trunks was two feet high. "Why aren't there any trees over there in the field?" asked Hannah, shielding her eyes from the sun.

"Those woods were burned by the Indians," explained Mother. "They do this so that grass will grow and become a meadow to attract deer. This was their hunting ground."

Along the edge of the forest they saw dandelions growing. The earlier settlers had brought this plant with them from Europe, and it had spread throughout the colonies. Hannah helped her mother gather the tender greens to cook for supper.

Growing nearby were sprouts with thick, pink stems. "Look, here's the poke berry plant," said Hannah.

"So it is," replied Mother. "And they'll grow much larger and be taller than you are by the end of the summer. We'll break off these now and stew them like asparagus. Later we can pick the top shoots and leaves to cook. But never eat the purple berries of the poke plant, Hannah," warned Mother. "They are poisonous. Birds can eat the seeds, but people can't."

Then Mother found some milk weeds growing in among the poke plants. "These are good to eat, too, with butter and salt,'' she said as she began to pick the leaves and buds at the tops of the plants. ''But we'll have to boil the greens several times, to get rid of the bitter.''

''No wonder it's called milk weed,'' cried Hannah. ''Look at my sticky, white hands,'' she said, holding them out for her mother to see.

Now Hannah and Mother made a path through the meadow. The warmth from the morning sun felt good on Hannah's shoulders. She felt as happy and care-free as the pretty yellow butterfly she was chasing across the field. Suddenly it came to rest upon another familiar looking plant. ''This looks like the water cress that grows down by the spring,'' she called, pointing to her discovery.

''Yes, Hannah, but this happens to be meadow cress. All of the cresses get their name from the four petals of the flowers. See, they're shaped in the form of a cross. But somehow people have changed cross to cress, and so we call it by that name instead.'' Both of them began to pick some of it for a salad.

When they had crossed over to the other side of the field, Mother stopped. She set her basket down and spied some blue violets growing beside a large rock.

''Can you eat violets?'' asked Hannah.

''Yes,'' her mother replied. ''Let's pick some of the greens for our salad.''

''The flowers are too pretty to eat,'' said Hannah nibbling on some of the leaves. While her mother sat down on the rock to rest for a while, Hannah continued to explore the forest edge, looking for wild strawberries. She found some plants but none in bloom yet.

By and by she came back to where her mother was sitting. All of a sudden Hannah saw something move in the leaves. She stopped and stood frozen still. There was a large snake coiled near the rock.

Hannah wanted to scream, but something told her not

to. A sudden noise would startle her mother, and the snake would surely strike. Hannah had to do something fast, but she remained motionless as though in a trance. Her heart pounded in her throat. At first she was too frightened to move—but when a noise like wind rattling through leaves came from the snake—she was too panic-stricken to stand still doing nothing.

Quickly looking around her, Hannah noticed a big stick within arm's reach. Ever so quietly she picked up the weapon and held it over her shoulder like a club. She could feel herself trembling.

With a hard swing, before she knew exactly what she was doing, Hannah brought the stick down on the snake's head as hard as she could, knocking it away from her mother.

"Hannah, whatever are you doing?" exclaimed Mother as she wheeled around at the sound.

Then seeing the snake writhing on the ground she gasped: "Oh, Hannah!" In a moment Hannah had run to her and was in her mother's arms.

"How brave, how very brave," her mother cried. "You've killed a rattler."

Hannah was shaking all over. "I—I didn't think I could do it, but I just had to," she sobbed. "It was going to bite you." Tears began to run down her face.

Mother kept her arms around Hannah. "It's all right, honey," she said. And then turning her head so that she might hear more clearly, "Listen, I think I hear Father's voice." Hannah listened, too. Now they could make out another noise in the distance. The squealing sound became more distinct.

Suddenly Mother began to laugh. "Jonathan must be chasing the wood hogs." Father had let the pigs out to feed on the roots, acorns, and beechnuts in the forest. Jonathan liked to run after them. And by now they could see the squealing pigs and hear the tinkling of their bells as they ran higgedly-piggedly through the woods.

"What if the pigs step on a rattler, Mother?" Hannah asked with the memory of the danger still vivid in her mind.

"A hog will usually kill a snake, Hannah. Besides, rattlers ordinarily can't hurt them because of their thick layer of fat. They just put their hoof on a snake and bite its head off."

Hannah shuddered. Wherever she looked, now, she imagined seeing a snake. "I hope Father and Jonathan don't come upon any," she thought.

When her father and brother reached them in the clearing, Mother told them what had happened. Father got down on his knees and turned the snake over.

"It's a big one all right," he said. Then he took a knife out of his pocket and cut the tail off and handed it to Hannah. Jonathan backed away. Hannah shivered as she counted the segments in her hand. There were nine rattles and a button. The snake that she had killed was almost four feet long, her father told her.

"A snake as long as that, Hannah, could kill a grown man with one strike," said Father. "That was quick thinking," he added. Hannah didn't say a word. She just stood there in a half-daze.

"Come along, Hannah," said Mother putting her arm around her. "Father and Jonathan can round up the rest of the pigs while we clean the greens."

Hannah followed her mother as she looked back at the snake lying on the ground. The mysterious woodland had revealed its secrets to her. There were all kinds of nice things to eat—"But it was sort of frightening, too," she thought. And somehow the forest and its wonder would never lose its enchantment for Hannah. Not even because of a snake.

# ix.

## *burrs and chestnuts*

THE AUTUMN WIND WHISTLED in the tall oak trees. Hannah could feel a cold draft coming in through every chink in the cabin walls. It was time to get chestnuts Winter was only a few weeks away, and if the nuts were not gathered soon, they would be lost under a blanket of snow.

The children hurriedly ate their favorite breakfast of pop-robin, which Mother made from eggs and flour boiled in milk. When they were finished they climbed up on the hard wooden wagon seat where Father and Shep were already waiting. This time Jonathan said, "Giddyup," just as he had heard Father say many times before. Father threw his head back and laughed heartily, as the horses jerked the wagon to a start.

Hannah and Jonathan looked up to see the wild geese honking their way south. Through a gap in the trees they got a glimpse of the great birds, flying so high that they were hardly more than dots in a "V" shape against the sky.

Close to the ground Hannah noticed some dry leaves dancing around in circles with the wind, like children at play.

In a short while they turned off the road into an open woodland with only a few bushes here and there.

After another mile, the way became so rough that Father got down and tied up the team to a sapling.

"From here on," he said, "we'll have to walk."

It was only a little way to the top of a knoll covered with a grove of chestnut trees, some of them very gnarled and old. Several gray squirrels fled at their approach, jumping from tree to tree. A few little red ones stayed close by.

Some of the chestnuts had already fallen from the opened burrs, but most of them still clung to the trees. While Hannah and Jonathan gathered what they could find on the ground, Father cut some large clubs.

"Now stand back so you won't be hit," he told them. "And be careful of the burrs. They can be mighty sharp."

As Father threw the clubs up into the tree, burrs and chestnuts came showering down like hail-stones. They could hardly wait until the last stick had hit the ground.

"Here's a big burr with some chestnuts still in it," called Jonathan as he ran under the tree. "Look what a fine one."

He picked it up and suddenly jerked his hand back. "Owwww!" he cried. In his haste he had forgotten the long spikes that covered the burrs. They had stuck in his thumb and fingers, and the burr dangled from them as he held up his hand. Jonathan had found out what Father meant.

Hannah looked at the burr that had stuck to her brother's fingers. She marveled at how prickly it was on the outside and yet the inside was as soft as the velvet on a deer's antler.

Jonathan was wailing with pain. "Here, let me look at it," said Father. He took Jonathan's hand and pulled the stickers out as gently as he could. Little drops of blood appeared, and Jonathan cried all the harder when he saw them.

"They do hurt a lot, Jonathan," said Father. "But it will be all right in a few minutes," he said as he kissed Jonathan's fingers.

"That feels better," said Jonathan. "But they still hurt," he sobbed.

"Come here, Jonathan," said Hannah. She put her arm around him, and they sat down on a fallen tree. "If you won't cry, I'll say 'Old Mrs. Maguire' for you."

Jonathan sobs gradually quieted as she recited the verse that Father had taught her:

Old Mrs. McGuire, she jumped in the fire.
The fire was so hot she jumped in the pot.
The pot was so black she jumped in a crack.
The crack was so high she jumped in the sky.
The sky was so blue she jumped in the canoe.
The canoe was so long she jumped in the pond.
The pond was so shallow she jumped in the tallow.
The tallow was so soft she jumped in the loft.
The loft was so rotten she jumped in the cotton.
The cotton was so white she stayed there all night
And never got a bite till the next daylight.

Jonathan was delighted. "Tell me more, Hannah," he begged. "Well," Hannah continued:

There was a man, and he went mad,
And he jumped into a pea-swad.
(That's a pea-pod, Jonathan,'' added Hannah.)
The pea-swad was over full,
So he jumped into a roaring bull.
The roaring bull was over fat,
So he jumped into a gentleman's hat.
The gentleman's hat was over fine,
So he jumped into a barrel of wine.
The bottle of wine was over dear,
So he jumped into a barrel of beer.
The barrel of beer was over the crick,
So he jumped into a clubstick.
The clubstick was over narrow,
So he jumped into a wheelbarrow.
The wheelbarrow began to crack,
So he jumped into a haystack.
The haystack began to blaze,
And he could do nothing but cough and sneeze.

By the time she had finished, Jonathan was laughing and had forgotten all about his hurt hand. He began to help Hannah pick up the chestnuts again. But she noticed he was careful not to try to get out the ones that were still stuck in the burrs.

At last the straw baskets were spilling over with the nuts that they had gathered. It was time to go home. ''We'll leave the rest for the squirrels and wild turkeys,'' said Father.

After supper, when the last dish was put away, Father suggested, ''Shall we roast some of our chestnuts?''

''Oh, let's,'' said Hannah with delight.

Father put some of the nuts onto a board placed as close to the logs as it could be without catching fire. Mother brought a wooden bowl full of apples they had been saving.

Sitting down on the long bench before the hearth she said, "Come Hannah, we can peel apples while we wait for the chestnuts to roast. And we'll have apple-sauce for breakfast, too."

"We might as well put a few apples to bake in front of the fire," said Father as he took some of the fruit from the bowl. He cut out the cores, and Mother put a lump of sugar in each apple.

Hannah helped her mother peel, core, and slice the apples. They saved the peelings to boil and make jelly.

"What kind of apples are these?" asked Hannah.

"They're pippins," replied Mother.

"That's a silly name," giggled Jonathan.

"Well, maybe there'll be an apple having your name some day, Jonathan," declared Hannah. "Would you like that better?"

"Oh, goodie, I hope so," her brother cried.

Just then a long peel from Hannah's apple dropped to the floor. Father quickly reached down and picked it up. Holding it in his hand, he asked, "Did you know that if you can peel an apple all over without letting the peeling break, you will have good luck?"

"And not only that, but if you throw it over your left shoulder, it will form the initial of the person you will marry someday," he went on.

Hannah took the apple peel and threw it just as Father had said. But no one could make out what initial it was. "Well, time will tell," said Father.

"Did you ever try this, Mother?" Hannah asked.

"Only once, a long time ago, and it formed the nicest 'D' you ever did see," she said, winking at Father.

After this Jonathan tried, too, but he was getting so many peelings all over the floor that Mother had to stop all of the fun.

When the apples were ready to be dried, Mother and

Hannah strung them on linen thread, and Father helped lift them onto the drying poles above the fireplace.

Some of the chestnuts now began to pop open. Father pulled the board back and began opening the leathery shells, blowing on them to cool them enough so they wouldn't burn the children's fingers.

"Mmmm, these are good," said Jonathan, "almost worth getting my fingers stuck."

Then he and Hannah began to recite "Old Mrs. McGuire" once more.

> "Old Mrs. McGuire, she jumped in the fire,
> The fire was so hot she jumped in the pot . . ."

When they had finished with the last line, and the apples and chestnuts had all been eaten, Mother drew them both close to her and hugged them. Then she kissed them good night saying:

> "And Hannah and Jonathan had both been fed,
> So now they had best jump into their bed."

# X.

# *big girl, little girl*

THE DAY WAS WARM for early April, and Hannah, if she wasn't exactly dallying, was certainly in no hurry about getting home. She had stayed for supper and spent the night at Jennifer's house. And now she was on her way home to help Mother with planting the garden.

It was the first time she had made the trip alone, and her parents had talked it over for quite a while before letting her stay with the Bradfords, whom they had seen in the blacksmith shop in Hanna's Town the afternoon before. Father and Mr. Bradford would be busy clearing some new ground  and wouldn't be able to give her a ride.

"Hannah's a big girl now," Father had finally decided. "She knows the way, and this is a safe and well-behaved neighborhood. After she gets to the main road there will almost always be a house within calling distance."

"There'll be a big crowd in town because of the court being in session," Mother had protested.

"Yes," said Father. "But we have never had any trouble on court days. That Dr. John Connelly who has taken over Fort Pitt and is trying to set up Virginia courts promised to appear for a hearing of the riot charges against him. But nobody believes he would risk facin' a Pennsylvania justice. Even if he should, all the attention would be on him. I think Hannah is big enough."

"Yes. I am a big girl now," Hannah kept thinking as she waved goodbye to Jennifer at the top of the hill and started walking along the Forbes Road that ran from Fort Pitt to Fort Ligonier. "And on to Fort Bedford, in the middle of the mountains," she thought, "and east for miles and miles and days and days until it gets to Lancaster, where we saw so many people who had big beards and funny clothes and talked a language we couldn't understand." Her mind rambled on.

There seemed to be nobody on the road today. She remembered Father telling her that it was getting very bad in the mountains for lack of work . . so bad that more things were moved over it by pack horses than by wagons. And people coming to court would all be there now and probably eating their dinners.

"How grand it would have been to see this road when it was first built," Hannah thought, "when all the soldiers and their wagons and cannons were coming over it to make the French give up Fort Duquesne, and build Fort Pitt in its place."

She was almost into Hanna's Town. But instead of its taverns and houses, she was seeing the great army of General John Forbes. It was so real that she could imagine she heard the pounding of the horses' hooves, the shouts of men, and the creaking of saddle leather.

All of a sudden she awoke to the fact that the sound wasn't coming from Fort Ligonier, as the great army had come, but from the direction of Fort Pitt, behind her.

"That isn't make-believe," Hannah gasped to herself. "This is real!"

Almost before she had time to get out of the road, the cavalcade was at hand. Except for a few officers, these men weren't dressed like soldiers. Most of them wore the long buckskin shirts of hunters and Indian traders. A few were dressed almost like Indians in just a loin cloth. They had long hair down to their shoulders and were sunburned almost as dark as natives. But they all carried rifles, and many of them wore the long, sharp blades that had caused the Indians to give Virginians the name "Long Knives."

"There must be a hundred of them," Hannah thought. "Maybe two hundred."

They were riding fast, crowding one another on the narrow road, shouting, and some of them cursing . . . something about "the Penns," and "teaching these Quakers a lesson." There was a big cloud of dust as they raced along.

When they reached the center of town, at Hanna's tavern, several of them reined up and fired their guns into the air. Hannah was so busy watching that she almost failed to see one of the riders pull his horse up beside her.

"Hey there, little girl," he called as he wheeled about. "Have ya' ever been to the other part of Virginy'?" And with that he reached down and tried to sweep Hannah off her feet. But somehow she managed to slip out of his arms.

Scared almost out of her wits, she fled through a gap between two hitching rails, and ducked around the back of the blacksmith shop.

"Never mind, girlie," he shouted after her. "I just wanted to scare ya'. Who'd want one of William Penn's people, anyway?" Hannah didn't stop, but ran down a side street until she came to Strawberry Alley where a woman was looking out of a cabin door.

"Those terrible men!" Hannah cried as she ran inside and hid. "Who are they? And why are they acting like that?"

"Take it easy, lass," said the woman in a strong Scottish brogue. "I think we're safe here. If I have me guess they're Lord Dunmore's ruffians . . . and I'm full of shame that a Scot would act so . . . they that have been stirrin' up trouble at Fort Pitt."

Peeping out from behind the door-jamb, Hannah could see enough to tell that the troop had made a circle around Hanna's tavern, which had been cleared out for court. A neighbor who passed by called out that they were refusing to let the justices enter. Dr. Connelly had announced that he was keeping his promise to appear, but that no Pennsylvania court was going to try him. And he read a long letter from Lord Dunmore, claiming the region west of the mountains for Virginia and placing him in charge of it.

"I think ye'd best not stir from here just noo, lassie," said the woman warmly.

Hannah thanked her. Suddenly she wasn't such a big girl, after all . . . just a little girl again, in a situation that frightened even the grown-ups.

"Can I do anything to help you while I'm here?" she asked.

The woman considered Hannah's offer.

"It wad help me a muckle if ye'd rock that cradle to keep the bairn from squallin' his head off while I'm scourin' this floor," she said.

Hannah hadn't even noticed the baby in her excitement, much less heard him till then. But she had often helped her mother when Jonathan was that little, and she knew what to do. She began rocking the cradle, and talking to the baby boy, who was less than a year old. Soon the child was cooing and clapping his hands.

Down on hands and knees, the woman was scrubbing the puncheon floor clean with white sand and water. An hour passed so quickly Hannah hardly thought of the time.

"It ought to be safe for ye to gae along noo," said the woman. She had just come back from a quick trip to another cabin. "Those ruffians have gane oot o'toon and threatened Mr. Hanna and another justice. There's still excitement, but I don't look for mair trouble the day."

Hannah thanked her again, threw a kiss to the baby, and started homeward as fast as her legs could carry her. As she turned onto the dusty highway, she almost ran into her father, looking very much worried. He had heard the news and come looking for her.

On the way home she told him everything that had happened and then had to tell it all over and over again for Mother and Jonathan.

"Just think what might have happened," said Mother with a worried look. "She could have been trampled to death or have been carried away."

"Well, she wasn't," said Father. "After all, Hannah is a big girl now and did just the right thing." But he looked very serious, too.

Hannah shivered at the thought of being kidnapped by such rough men.

"Oh, that terrible fellow," she complained. "What he said!"

"What did he say?" asked Mother in alarm.

"He called me a little girl!"

# xi.

# *snowbound*

DECEMBER CHILL WAS IN the air. Mother had just cleared the table, given the bones off the plates to Shep, and washed the supper dishes. She then mixed the leaven for bread and let it settle until morning.

Hannah was drying and putting the dishes back on the shelf as she listened to the wind howling outside the smoke-filled cabin.

Near the fireplace, Father was whittling out an axe handle from a piece of hickory. As he worked, he whistled a little tune.

Jonathan, sprawled at his feet, was catching the curly shavings as they fell onto the floor. Shep lay nearby chewing on a few of the ones that he missed.

"You can tell a glutton by his bones, and a workman by his chips," said Father with a twinkle in his eyes. He continued whistling.

Hannah was putting the last earthenware bowl away when Mother said, "Hannah, fetch some fresh butter from the firkin in the spring house for tomorrow's breakfast."

Firkin

Pulling her cloak tightly around her shoulders, Hannah went to do as she was told. It was getting colder outside, and now snowflakes were starting to fall.

Hannah ran back into the cabin with a bowl of butter. Her head was white. "It's snowing heavier than I've ever seen it!" she cried excitedly.

Father stopped whistling and got up to look out the door. Dark clouds were gathering in the sky. Night was falling fast.

"It looks like a big storm is movin' in from the southwest," said Father as he peered outside. "That's where we get our heavy snows."

Father was right, for the next morning Hannah was awakened by something falling on her as she lay sleeping snugly in the loft. She opened her eyes and felt her face. There was cold, wet snow on her cheek. It was sifting down through every tiny crack in the roof.

Hannah's breath seemed to freeze in the air. Her nose prickled with the cold. She moved her covers aside and got up from her mattress of corn husks.

As Hannah climbed down from the loft, she could see Mother shivering over by the fireplace. It had turned bitter cold during the night.

"The snow had made everything so quiet, we slept until the fire went out," Mother said.

The lid of the metal tinder box near the fireplace was open. It was filled with wood shavings, splinters, twigs, and lint scraped off worn-out linen clothing. Father was kneeling before a tiny pile of tow. He was striking a piece of steel against a flint to make sparks. Each time that he struck the flint he leaned over and very gently blew on the tuft of tinder, trying to get a flame started. He worked at it hard, for he didn't want to have to make his way to the nearest neighbor's for some hot coals on a strip of green bark to start the fire.

Finally on the third or fourth try, a strong spark caused the tinder to glow. Quickly Father placed a little splinter of wood on it and gently blew again. Very carefully he put a few more splinters on, one at a time. Then he added some wood shavings. A flame flickered up. The shavings had caught fire. Hannah watched as Father broke up some twigs and put them on top of the flames.

"Now, that should do it," Father said as he placed a small split log on the fire.

Hannah went to the door and tried to open it. She pushed and pushed, but the snow had drifted against the door, and she could only move it a crack.

Peeping outside, Hannah saw a strange world before her. The fields were completely covered with a deep blanket of snow. At the edge of the silent woods, the serviceberry branches looked like piles of feather pillows. The boughs of the fir trees by the spring house were bent to the ground with the weight of the snow upon them.

Hannah could no longer tell where the road was. She

looked up into the morning sky. Snow was still falling steadily all around, but now the flakes were tiny instead of the big ones she had seen last night.

"I'll get the snow away from the door after breakfast," said Father. "Now, at least we'll be warm." He added another log to the crackling fire.

Jonathan began stirring in his trundle bed. "Jonathan, look outside," said Hannah.

Her brother rubbed his eyes and sleepily wandered over to the door. "Oh, such a lot of snow," he said as he peeped out the crack. "It must be as high as I am." Jonathan began to hop and dance around the cabin floor in his nightshirt. They all burst out laughing. This was the most snow that he had ever seen.

Mother neatly folded Jonathan's deer skin cover and pushed his bed back out of the way under the larger one.

Hannah went over to dip out some water from the wooden bucket sitting on a bench. She looked over the rim to see inside. The water was frozen on the surface. Mother came and broke the ice with a wooden spoon and began to stir up some buckwheat batter.

"I'm afraid we're going to be snowbound," she said anxiously looking at the logs beside the fireplace.

Father noticed her glance over in that direction. "If it keeps on snowing all season the way it's been so far, the wood pile outside may not last. Might have to cut more wood," he said. Mother still seemed to be concerned over the snow.

And then Father added with a more cheerful note: "But a snowy winter means a plentiful harvest."

Hannah knew what snowbound meant. She had remembered her mother telling about another severe blizzard that they had had before she was born. Now Hannah knew that she might not be able to see Jennifer for a long, long time.

The smell of buckwheat cakes began to fill the room.

"Put some maple syrup into a bowl, Hannah," said Mother as she tended the pancakes. The sausage sizzled over the fire.

In no time at all the cakes were stacked on the table beside the browned meat from the hog that Father had butchered a week ago. The syrup was so cold it would hardly pour. There was plenty of fresh butter that Hannah had gotten the night before. Mother heated some spiced cider in an iron kettle over the fire.

Hannah was hungry. And the melted butter flowing with the sweet syrup on the pancakes tasted good. For a few minutes everyone was too busy eating to talk.

"Now," said Father taking a piece of bread and wiping his trencher clean, "the animals must be fed." Pushing back his bench, he got up from the table and walked over to the door. Father put on his leather shoepacks and reached for his great coat hanging from a peg on the wall.

When he was ready, Father put his shoulder to the door and forced it open enough that he could push out a broomstick and scrape away some of the snow. Then by scraping and sweeping he got it open halfway, enough to step outside.

A gust of frosty air blew inside the cabin. Father began to tramp his way to the shed where the animals were kept.

"Come along, Hannah," he called after him, "I need you to help me with the chores."

Hannah usually went with her father to milk Daisy and to help feed the horses and chickens. She quickly slipped into her shoepacks, warm hooded cloak, and woolen mittens. She pushed the door open and shut it behind her to keep that cabin warm.

Outside, the snow was almost up to her waist. The wind whipped Hannah about as she walked in the footprints that Father had made, although she had to stretch her legs to step into his big footprints. It was snowing so hard now that Hannah could hardly see where she was going. When she reached the shed, Father had a wooden pitch fork in his hands and was already throwing hay to the horses. The animals whinnied when they saw her.

"Go ahead and get started with the milking, Hannah," said Father. "But be sure to leave enough milk for the calf to drink."

Hannah knew just what to do. First she carefully wiped off all the bits of straw and dirt from the cow's udder. Then she found the three-legged stool that Father had made for her. After seating herself upon it beside Daisy, Hannah began to milk. She placed the bucket between her knees. Her hands knew the rhythm of milking the cow. Right—left. Right—left. Squirt, squirt went the milk into the bucket. The calf bawled loudly in the next stall. Daisy continued to munch on her hay.

Hannah's cat and four little kittens ambled over to where she was sitting. The kittens tumbled over one another, trying to get closer. Hannah squirted one of them in the face with the creamy milk. The kitten licked it off with her tiny pink tongue. Hannah laughed.

Here, kitty," she said. This time she did it again on purpose. Now the mother cat and all her brood eagerly sat around Hannah and mewed as they waited their turn.

Hannah didn't take all of Daisy's milk, for her calf still had to drink. She hung the milk pail on a bracket made from a forked bough and turned the calf into the stall with its mother. The calf began to drink hungrily, nudging Daisy's flank with its head now and then.

Finding a piece of a broken crock nearby, Hannah poured some of the foam from the milk pail into it. Now the cat and her kittens gathered around, circling in and out between Hannah's legs, purring, and lapping up the milk.

The next chore was to feed the chickens pecking around her feet and wanting to be fed, too.

The snow continued to fall almost all day. It was too deep even for pack horses to get over the roads.

That night was very cold. The family huddled around the fire to keep warm. The firelight cast strange shadows that danced upon the cabin walls.

"Well, there's one thing we don't have to worry about," said Father. "The Indians would never attack us in this kind of weather."

The once peaceful Indians had been stirred up so much lately by Dr. John Connelly and his ruffians, that Colonel Arthur St. Clair had advised the settlers in Hanna's Town to build a fort for protection.

"And we don't have to think about taking refuge in the fort now," he continued.

Hannah remembered how she and Jennifer had watched with excitement as the men constructed the two-room cabin fort on a high point of level land one day. It had a nearly flat roof and no windows on the upper story. But there were small port holes on the second floor through which rifles could be pushed.

"Well, since it's a still time, we needn't be concerned over the Indians," said Mother brightly. "I haven't felt so safe in a long time. Let's enjoy our evening."

Father got up and walked across the room. He took *Poor Richard's Almanac* off the shelf. Father read to the family until he came to the line, "Early to bed and early to rise; makes a man healthy, wealthy and wise."

Before he had a chance to read further, Mother interrupted: "Since it's too early for us to go to bed yet, let's tell riddles."

"Fine idea," agreed Father as he closed the book. After a moment of thought he asked: "Does anyone know this one? A house full, a hole full, you can't catch a bowl full."

The family thought and thought.

"I wonder what it could be?" pondered Hannah. No one seemed to know.

"Do you want me to tell you now?" asked Father good naturedly.

"Yes, yes," cried Jonathan with excitement.

"All right. The answer is smoke."

"Oh, why didn't I think of that," complained Hannah.

"Now, I have one," said Mother. "What is tall as a pine and slim as a pumpkin vine?" After they had thought for a while and no one came up with the right answer, Mother said, "I'll give you a clue. It looks like a snake, too."

Hannah had a puzzled look on her face and then she lit up with a smile. "I know," she said. "It must be rope."

"That's right," said Mother. "Now you ask a riddle."

Hannah remembered one that Father had told her once before. "Crooked as a snake and has teeth like a cat. Whatever you guess, you can't guess that."

Father kept silent while Mother and Jonathan tried to think of the answer. When they finally gave up, Hannah said: "It's a greenbrier."

'Ohhh," they both moaned.

"Now, how about you, Jonathan," suggested Hannah. "Do you know one?"

Jonathan thought for a while and then asked: "What's white and it's cold like ice?"

Hannah shrugged her shoulders, and Jonathan impatiently cried: "Snow, snow, don't you know!" And he began to dance around the room once more.

"You're a poet, Jonathan, and you don't even know it," laughed Hannah. She was having so much fun that she almost forgot how cold she was and hardly noticed the roar of the wind blowing the snow outside.

"Well," said Mother when no one could think of another riddle, "it's been a long time since we've heard any music around here.'' She looked over in Father's direction. Mother didn't have to say another word. Father went to the shelf and took down his treasured fiddle. After putting rosin on his bow, he tuned up.

Father began to play as Hannah, Mother, and Jonathan danced and sang along with him.

> A penny for a spool of thread,
> A penny for a needle,
> That's the way the money goes,
> Pop! goes the weasel.

> All around the cobbler's bench,
> The monkey chased the weasel,
> The monkey thought 'twas all in fun,
> Pop! goes the weasel.

> Potatoes for an Irishman's taste,
> A doctor for the measles,
> A fiddler always for a dance,
> Pop! goes the weasel.

At last when they were all out of breath and could play and dance no longer, Mother brought a loaf of bread and a crock of blackberry jam over to the table. She had baked that day while Hannah and Father were doing the chores.

Mother began to slice the loaf. All of a sudden Jonathan stammered, ''I-I don't want any!''

Then Mother, looking quite surprised, placed both hands on her hips and said, ''Well, I declare, no wonder you're not hungry, Jonathan.'' There was a small hole poked through the side of the bread. Jonathan had gouged out all the freshly baked dough and had eaten it. Only the crusty shell was left. Inside there was nothing but air.

Father tried very hard not to chuckle, and Hannah turned away so that Mother wouldn't see her snickering. Mother said sternly: "This had better never happen again, young man, or you'll get your hide tanned!"

Then Hannah glanced at Father, and Father in turn looked up at Mother. But Mother was still frowning at Jonathan. Suddenly they all burst out laughing. They laughed and laughed until they could laugh no more. When at last they had stopped, Hannah groaned: "Ooooh! My sides are hurting." She doubled over as if she were in pain.

"Mine are, too," said Mother. "I haven't laughed this hard since the time that Jonathan poured the maple syrup into Father's shoepacks." Hannah held her sides, and they all started to laugh once more.

Father then gave Jonathan a quick swat across the seat of his pants and sent him scampering off to bed. "See you in the morning, son," he said with a smile.

Hannah went up to the loft soon after her brother. She took all of the clothes that she owned off the pegs on the wall and piled them on top of her bed to keep her warm. But all the homespun garments could not shut out the chill of that bitter, cold night.

The West family were snowbound for two weeks, and Father's wood pile did last until the end of the winter.

**Wooden Pitchfork**

# xii.

## *syrup and surprises*

IT WAS THE THIRD month of the year. Winter was all but over now. The frosty nights were followed by sunny days, and the flow of the sap in the sugar maple trees was well on its way.

Today was a special one for Hannah. It was her tenth birthday. But Hannah was happy for another reason, too. Father had promised that she and Jennifer could go to the woods with him on the second day of the maple syrup season. During the winter months Mr. Bradford and Father had whittled enough spiles for the sap to run through out of elder or bourtree wood and had tapped the trees the day before. They had placed wooden buckets, or keelers, as Father called them, under the spiles to collect the sap.

Since Mr. Bradford had to go into Hanna's Town to get salt from the pack train that had just arrived from Fort

Ligonier, the girls would help Father boil the sap and tend
fire today.

In the early morning just before sunrise, they started
out. Shep ran ahead barking and romping in the snow. It
was so cold that they could see their breath in the frozen
air. The snow still lay deep in the woods and at times
touched the horses' bellies. But Hannah felt warm and
snug in the new red woolen scarf and mittens that Mother
had knitted for her birthday.

The horse-drawn sled had made the same journey the
day before with all the things that were needed: an iron
kettle, wooden buckets, an axe, a long wooden spoon, and
a yoke for carrying the sap buckets.

Today the sled carried Father and two very anxious
girls who could hardly wait to get to the maple grove.

Father looked up into the lacey snow-covered branches
along the way. "What would we ever do without trees?"
he mused. "We get everything imaginable from them.
Everything from fence posts to kindling wood."

"And our cabins and furniture," added Hannah.

"Our sleds and wagons, too," said Jennifer.

"Fruits, nuts, and birch bark tea," reminded Hannah.

"And now here we are on our way to get maple sugar
from them," said Father as he snapped the reins on the
horses.

"They sure are pretty," said Hannah looking up at the
naked, white branches. She remembered the brilliant red
and yellow leaves that were on them at harvest time. And
she knew how much Father loved trees.

From the winding road the girls could see the rocky
hillside covered with the sugar maples.

"Gee," said Father as he commanded the horses to turn
to the right. Then he called, "Haw," and they veered to
the left. In another moment they were there.

The girls could see the rough lean-to that Father and Mr. Bradford had built yesterday to keep off the wind.

Father's leather shoepacks crunched in the snow as he went from tree to tree checking the spiles they had placed the day before.

As he did so, he explained to the girls how a tree is tapped. "The lower ya' tap, the more tha' sap," he said with a smile.

"We learned how to tap trees and make maple syrup from the Indians," he went on. "They slash the trees with a tomahawk and let the sap drip down into a hollow cut in the tree. But this is hard on trees and in time will kill'em. It's much better to bore a hole and fit it with a hollow reed to drip from."

While they waited for the sun to make the sap flow more, Father cut down some dead trees and chopped them up. "You girls can help by gathering thick, dry branches." Hannah and Jennifer obeyed without further delay and began to collect more wood. Shep playfully snapped at the snow-covered limbs they dragged along to where Father was chopping them up with his axe.

Father started the fire under a large black kettle that was hanging from a pole resting on two forked ironwood saplings he had driven into the ground. He attached two keelers of maple sap to the ends of a wooden yoke around his neck, and carried them over to the fire. The buckets hanging from short ropes, swayed from side to side as he walked.

While the girls waited for the sap to boil they warmed themselves by the fire. They liked to poke it with a stick and watch the sparks fly about.

"Mind that you don't get too close and get burned," warned Father as he tended the sweet smelling sap.

The sun was high in the sky. "Who's hungry?" asked

Father at last. It had taken all morning to gather enough wood to keep the sap boiling.

Hannah and Jennifer were ready to eat. Mother had packed slices of smoked ham, rolls, doughnuts, apples, and a jug of cider for them. Father warmed the cider in a pot over the fire and fried the ham. The girls had sampled so much of the cold sap from the maple trees that they were not very thirsty. But the hot drink made them feel warm all over.

While they ate, Father told more stories.

"The Indians use birch buckets to gather the sap," he said. "But they can't put these over the fire, for they would burn. So, in order to boil the sap, they heat stones until they are red-hot and drop them one at a time into a bucket, with twig tongs. When one stone cools down, they have another one ready in order to keep the syrup boiling."

"Wouldn't that take a lot of time?" asked Hannah.

"Yes, but since they usually don't have iron kettles, this is the only way they can do it," explained her father.

"I'm sure glad that you have a kettle, Mr. West," said Jennifer.

Father and Hannah laughed as they agreed with her.

"Sometimes they will freeze the juice and when the ice forms they throw it away, leavin' the thick maple syrup in the bottom," Father went on.

"Why isn't there any syrup in the ice?" asked Hannah.

"Because the sugar doesn't freeze," answered Father.

When the sugar water boiled down to where it was thick as honey, Father took a big wooden spoon and dipped some of the hot syrup out of the kettle onto the snow.

"Why are you doing that?" asked Jennifer in surprise.

"Just watch and see what happens now," returned Father.

To their amazement the girls saw the syrup cool and harden in the snow. Father reached down and picked up lumps of maple candy. He handed pieces to the girls and kept some for himself.

"Mmmmm, this is good. But why doesn't the sap from the trees taste sweet, too?" asked Hannah.

"There's a legend that once upon a time the sap from maple trees tasted as thick and as sweet as pure maple syrup," said Father. "But people wasted it. The great Indian spirit, Ne-naw-bo-zhoo, realized this and decided that something that good should not come too easy. So he made the sugar-water nearly tasteless, and people had to work hard to enjoy it."

Hannah and Jennifer laughed over the legend.

"Well, at least one thing is true," said Hannah. "It's not easy."

Soon it was near the end of the afternoon. The girls helped Father strain the syrup through a piece of flannel cloth to get out any leaves or dirt that might have fallen into it. Then they put out the fire with some snow. Tomorrow Father and Mr. Bradford would continue with the maple syrup making. And then for days and on into nights until they were finished.

Mother greeted them when they arrived home. They stamped the snow off their shoepacks and shook their clothing. Father poured all of the maple syrup they had brought back into the big black kettle in the fireplace above blazing logs that Mother had ready for them.

Jennifer was invited to stay all night since it was Hannah's birthday. The girls helped get the meal ready while the syrup bubbled and boiled once more over the fire.

"After supper there'll be plenty of time to sugar off," Mother said to the girls as they set the table. "We'll ladle

the syrup into buckets to cool until morning. And
tomorrow there'll be a big cake of solid sugar in each
one."

The syrup that Father would bring home on the last day
of the maple sugaring would not be boiled down as this was
today. Mother would pour that syrup into jugs to be stored
for eating with pancakes.

At last supper was ready. The children washed their
hands in a wooden pail with soap that Mother had made.
They sat down around the table. Everyone bowed their
heads as Father gave the blessing:

> The Lord is only my support,
> And he that doth me feed,
> How can I then want anything,
> Whereof I stand in need.

Hannah said the grace to herself, for she knew it by
heart. It was from *Pilgrim's Progress*, and Father had a
habit of saying it at every meal time.

On the table were a plump loaf of freshly baked bread,
spicy apple butter, smoked pork, cooked dried peas,
steaming hot turnips, and a jar of honey that Mother had
purchased from a trader in town. Father was in a jovial
mood and said:

> Oh, I eat my peas with honey,
> I've done it all my life,
> It makes my food taste funny,
> But they stay upon my knife.

Caught up in the spirit of the moment, Jennifer said,
"Here's another rhyme. Only this one is especially for
Hannah.

> A riddle, a riddle, I suppose,
> A thousand eyes, and never a nose.

Know what it is, Hannah?" asked Jennifer eagerly.

Hannah thought for a while and so did the rest of the family. Finally Jennifer reached into her pocket and pulled out something shiny. It was a tiny brass thimble. She handed it to her friend. "This is for you, Hannah," Jennifer said a bit shyly. "For your birthday."

Hannah looked at her companion. "Oh, Jenny! Thank you," she beamed with admiration. "I never had a thimble of my own before. And it does have lots of eyes, just as the riddle says."

Hannah turned the thimble over and over in her hand. "Oh, and look, there's something written around the rim," she exclaimed. "It says, 'Forget Me Not'." Hannah looked up, her face alight with joy and excitement. "How could I ever forget you, Jenny?"

She was sure she never would.

"Oh, could we please play 'Thimble, Thimble, Who's Got the Thimble'?" asked Hannah eagerly turning to her mother.

"Well," paused Mother. "Since it is your birthday, I guess we can," she consented.

"Here, Mother, you be 'it' first," said Hannah, holding out her gift.

Even Father joined in to have enough to make it interesting. Mother held the thimble out of sight while all the others put their hands in front of them to hide it if she passed it to them.

Then she went all around the circle, twice, slipping her hands between theirs, and out again, saying: "Hold all I give you."

Mother turned to Jennifer, "Thimble; thimble, who's got the thimble?" she asked. "If you have it, it's all right to say that someone else has it, just for the game," she explained.

"Hannah has it," said Jennifer. "I can see it in her eyes."

Then Mother asked Hannah. "Does Father have it?" Father was sure Hannah had it, and Jonathan declared that Jennifer had it.

"Rise, thimbler, rise," said Mother at last. Jonathan proudly stood up and displayed it. Because nobody had guessed him, he became the next "it".

When the game was over, Mother announced, "Now for another surprise." Getting up from the table, she went to the cupboard and brought back a bowl of pudding that she had made especially for Hannah.

"I helped make it, Hannah," Jonathan piped up proudly.

"He certainly did at that," said Mother with a smile. "And when I wasn't looking, Jonathan added a special touch to your pudding."

Mother brought the bowl over to where Hannah was sitting. She set it down in front of her. And there on the very top was printed the name, JONATHAN WEST, in big letters. Jonathan had placed raisins on the pudding, spelling out his full name.

Everyone began to laugh. "I said you would learn how to spell your name right some day, Jonathan. I just knew you could do it," declared Hannah with pride. "That's the nicest present you could have given me."

Mother took a wooden spoon and gave each of them a serving. Hannah still held onto her brass thimble. She began to eat her pudding. This was the best birthday she had ever had.

# xiii.

## *the hanna's town resolves*

Hᴀɴɴᴀʜ's ʜᴇᴀʀᴛ ᴘᴏᴜɴᴅᴇᴅ ᴡɪᴛʜ every beat of the drums each time there was a muster at the Hanna's Town fort. There was much activity and excitement in the colonies during the year 1775. It had been four weeks since the British had fought with the Americans at Lexington, Massachusetts. Wherever Hannah went she could hear the grown-ups talking about the trouble with England.

The words, "taxation without representation" were spoken quite often. Hannah didn't know exactly what they meant, but she did know that it was disturbing the townsfolk. Even before this, the people of the village had been restless. There had been border disputes. And some of the settlers were uncertain whether to stay or leave. Many had not bothered to plow or sow their fields that spring.

Only three months ago some of Connelly's men, led by

Ben Harrison, had ridden into Hanna's Town again. This time it was in the wee hours of the morning before anyone was up. They raided the blacksmith shop and stole hammers and irons to break open the jail.

Judge Hanna had tried to stop them, but they only jeered at him and released all the prisoners. Then at the end of that same month he and Judge Cavett were arrested and imprisoned in Pittsburgh, merely because they were leaders under the Penn family.

Now the excitement was centered around England. Instead of Lord Dunmore of Virginia, now the mother country was raising trouble. Everyone wanted to unite and take action against the British tyrants.

Mr. Bradford and Hannah's father had gone to the meeting at the court house to help decide what to do about the situation. The meeting had actually started yesterday, on the sixteenth of May, the same day Pittsburgh held one of the same kind. The people of Hanna's Town continued their discussion to the second day to finish drawing up some resolutions.

Jennifer's father had dropped her off at Hannah's house that morning before going to the meeting.

"Let's go pick some May apple blossoms," suggested Hannah after they had eaten. Jennifer agreed, and the girls started out for the high hill overlooking Hanna's Town. All of the talk about war with England was very distressing. Hannah was worried about what would happen next.

"I wonder if there'll be fighting here, too?" she said out loud to Jennifer.

"Oh, I hope not," answered her friend. "There's been shooting in the northern colonies. Dr. Connelly has stirred the Indians up terrible, too. They might cause trouble."

The girls found a quiet spot where the ground was

completely covered with May apples. They tried to talk of other things, but somehow they couldn't get their minds off the important meeting that day.

"It's a good thing that we have a fort here," said Hannah straightening up after picking a handful of May apple leaves and blossoms. Looking over the hillside in the direction of the stockade she added, "If the British do come here, we can run into the fort and be safe."

"That's right, Hannah," replied Jennifer more cheerfully now. "So what are we worried about?"

The girls had been so busy talking that they walked further down the hill than they realized. They had just reached town when they could see a crowd of people at the courthouse tavern a short distance away.

Hannah and Jennifer soon became a part of the crowd. They moved in among the motley throng of spectators, farmers in home-spun garments, and hunters in buckskin all clamoring for action.

The crowd became noisy and excited. The girls could see that the meeting was going to be a hectic one. By now there were so many people that they decided to hold it out under the trees.

A gentleman got up to speak. "Sinclair will get things settled," the girls heard a man beside them murmur. Hannah and Jennifer nudged each other as they giggled at hearing Colonel Arthur St. Clair spoken of in such a way.

He began in a loud, clear voice to address the crowd, but the girls still couldn't hear all that was said over the noise of the boisterous townspeople. They elbowed their way up front. People hardly noticed them as they were swallowed up by the mob.

"At least this time we won't have to eavesdrop," whispered Hannah to her friend. "We're right in the middle of it."

"Look, so are the Hanna girls," said Jennifer pointing out Robert Hanna's daughters, who were in the midst of the excitement, too.

The girls listened to the hurly-burly of the crowd. "I reckon we're headed for war," one of the men said.

"Aye, sometimes a man has ta' fight for what he thinks is right," another answered. Hannah felt a chill go through her. It was all so very frightening.

Then someone began to read the resolves that were drawn up. The girls caught the words, " . . . as for us we will oppose it with our lives and fortunes." The people of Hanna's Town were going to pledge their loyalty to King George III, but at the same time blamed England for its tyranny. And if the mother country refused to listen to them, they were willing to fight.

"We can make our own laws. England must listen to us. We're free men," someone proclaimed loudly.

A cheer arose and there was more yelling and shouting. The patriots continued to state their grievances, and the rest of the resolutions were written down in the shade of the great forest.

When Hannah heard that a military unit would be formed, the man next to her said to his companion, "And we ought ta' have a special flag for our militia, too. One that'll make the British sit up and take notice."

At last the meeting adjourned, and a notice was posted on a tree that the next gathering would be on the twenty-fourth of the month to decide on officers. Hanna's Town's little declaration was made known far and wide. The news spread throughout the county.

When the meeting broke up, Hannah and Jennifer were pushed about and stepped upon in all the excitement of the mob. As Colonel Proctor brushed by them, the girls heard him murmur, "What may be the fate of this country, God only knows!"

When they at last worked their way free from the crowd, they spied their fathers' horses tied to a hitching post outside the courthouse tavern. The girls waited to get a ride home.

Soon after they reached home there was a call outside the West cabin, and Hannah saw Colonel St. Clair on his big gray horse. Father went out and they talked very seriously.

"I'm as much afraid of success in this contest as I am of being vanquished," said St. Clair. "They're blaming it all on the Parliament now. But soon they will include the King, and next be demanding independence. That will mean war, I fear."

Father returned to the cabin, his brow knit with worry. Hannah had heard the conversation, and she was troubled, too. But at least she was glad to be home and away from the wild mob.

Hannah had been so lost in thought that she had completely forgotten about her May apple blossoms. They had all wilted, clutched tightly in her hand.

And in spite of the excitement, Old Bob and Bessie and even Daisy, the cow, continued to munch peacefully on the clover as if nothing had happened that day. And the May apples blossoming on the hillside paid no mind to what was said.

# xiv.

## *thimble, thimble*

"PLEASE PASS ME THE blue thread, Jenny," said Hannah. "I'm ready to change colors now." Hannah and Jennifer were working on their samplers inside the West cabin.

A few minutes later Hannah gave a sigh of relief. "There," she said. "It's finished at last." She spread out her needlework for Jennifer to see.

"Forsake not a friend," Jennifer read. "Hannah, that's beautiful."

"That saying comes from the middle of the Bible, between the old part and the new, in Ecclesiasticus," said Hannah.

As they were talking, Hannah's cat and her new litter of kittens were playing with a ball of yarn near Mother's spinning wheel. Just then one of the kitten's scurried over and tried to catch some of Hannah's embroidery thread with its paw. The kitten's claw caught a strand. "Shoo, kitty," said Hannah as she gently brushed it aside.

The kitten bounded away, but not before the brass thinble, the one that Jennifer had given Hannah, fell from her lap. It dropped to the floor and rolled along until it came to a knot hole in a board. Down it went and out of sight.

"Oh, dear," cried Hannah. She jumped up and ran to the spot where it had disappeared. Kneeling down on her hands and knees and peering into the opening, she tried to look for the thimble. But the darkness concealed it, and it was lost in the shadows.

"My thimble," cried Hannah in disbelief. "Maybe Father will take up the floor board for me. Oh, I do hope that I can get it back."

All of a sudden they could hear the sound of horse's hooves on the path leading to the cabin.

"It's your father, Jenny," said Hannah getting up from the floor and looking out the door. "I guess he's come for you."

Hannah's father was outside making a scarecrow for the cornfield.

"Here's a letter for you, Dan," Mr. Bradford said, holding it out in his hand. "Bob Hanna just gave it to me when I came through town. It came by the same messenger that brought the news about Lexington, but with so much excitement he'd forgotten all about it till now."

Father quickly took the letter and tore off the wax seal. After reading the message, he slowly looked up at Mother, who was anxiously waiting to hear what the news was. Hannah knew that it must be something important, for it was unusual to receive a letter.

"What's the matter, Father?" Hannah questioned soberly.

"It's from your Grandmother West," Father said. His eyes returned to the sheet of paper in his hand.

"Dear ones," he began,

"It saddens me to have to bring this news to you at such a time. There seems to be enough trouble, the colonies quarreling with England, and so much unrest everywhere. And now to add to our woe, Grandfather West is quite ill and needs help with the farm. He didn't want me to write to you about it, but I felt that I must.

"It has been so long since we have seen you. Father and I miss you all so very much . . ."

Father stopped reading and handed the letter to Mother. Their eyes met. She re-read it to herself and slowly tucked it away in her apron pocket.

"We must go back, Rebecca," said Father at last. "They need us. I'm afraid that there'll be hard times ahead. The news of Lexington and now this. Perhaps it is best if we do return. As soon as Britain hears that we're fightin' for our freedom, they'll get the Indians against us here on the frontier. And you know how frightening the Indian summers are."

Hannah knew that the Indians, when stirred up, usually attacked in the summer or fall, rather than in the winter time.

"And we're right where the Indians will be on the war path. There's no telling what will happen once this occurs," he added.

"You're right, Dan," spoke up Mr. Bradford. "I've been thinking about leavin', too, but I just can't quite make up my mind. Now that my family is settled and the fields are all cleared, I just hate to pull up stakes and leave.

"But on the other hand," he said, "I'm sort of anxious to find more open space again. It's starting to get crowded in Hanna's Town. When you can see the smoke from your neighbor's chimney down the road from you, it's time to be movin' on, so they say.''

Hannah didn't want to hear any more. "Come on, Jenny, let's go up on the hillside." While their fathers continued talking, Jennifer laid her sewing aside and joined Hannah.

They climbed the hill together, not saying a word for some time. Finally Hannah broke the silence. "I just can't believe it. How could we leave? This is our home. I love Hanna's Town. I want to stay here forever, no matter what happens. The Indians are our friends. They wouldn't turn against us. I just know they won't," she said remembering the string of shell beads that the Indian had given her down by the spring house. But in her heart she knew that already they had been troublesome.

Then she wondered about her father's orchard that he had planted. Who would eat all the apples someday and tell fortunes with them?

They had reached the top of the hill now. "Jenny, I may not be able to see you any more," said Hannah. It suddenly dawned upon her that moving from Hanna's Town would also mean leaving her friend behind. Jenny—whom she had met in the blackberry patch one day in the spring. Jenny—who had given her a brass thimble. And oh! How pretty it was, but now it was gone.

From the top of the hill they could see a farmer riding along with a load of hay. Hannah slowly said out loud,

> Hay, hay, a load of hay,
> Make a wish and turn away.

How many times before she had heard her mother say that little rhyme and she had laughed at it. But now she didn't. She just closed her eyes and made a wish. "Oh, I do hope that Jennifer will never forget me," she thought.

Hannah felt sad and torn inside. A slight breeze was blowing through the oak trees on top of the hill. She and Jennifer looked down over the village of Hanna's Town. They had climbed this hillside many times together. Long summer days they had sat on the brow of the hill making dolls out of hollyhock flowers and weaving daisy chains. They had picked May apples from its sides. And they had rolled down its slopes, tumbling after one another, with the blue sky and green grass going round and round in a blur of dizzy circles as they went.

But now Hannah and her family would be leaving. It just didn't seem possible. "Maybe we'll move, too, Hannah," said Jennifer slowly and somewhat hopefully.

Hannah took in the view of the rooftops on the log cabins nestled below in the trees. Her eyes came to rest on the fort that they had watched the men build the year before. Hannah looked across the rolling hills, rye fields and patches of flax with its blue blossoms. A lump suddenly came up in her throat as she tried to choke back the tears.

Daylight was nearly gone now and it would soon be supper time. Jennifer's father would be ready to go home. The girls turned to go back down the hillside. There was a sudden change in the wind. Great drops of rain began to fall in the dust on the path.

Hannah knew that they would be packing soon to make the long journey over the mountains. Of course it would be nice seeing her grandparents, but it was hard to leave, too. "I think I know how a weed feels when it's pulled up by the roots," she thought.

"Here, Jenny, I want you to have this," Hannah said suddenly, holding out her sampler when they arrived at the cabin. It wasn't the first time that she had given her needlework away.

"Oh, I couldn't take it," said Jennifer. But after a

moment she did, clutching it tight. "Hannah, I'll always be a faithful friend."

"I know you will, Jenny," said Hannah. Both had tears in their eyes.

In the course of time, Hannah and her family packed their necessary belongings and got ready to move. They sold what they could, and Mr. Bradford was going to look after the farm and try to find a buyer.

"It won't be easy with all this trouble," he said. "But there's always somebody comin' west. I'll do the best I can."

The goodbyes had all been said the night before, and early in the morning Father hitched up the horses at the crack of dawn. By good daylight they were on their way. Jonathan was so much excited over his first long trip that he hardly realized they were leaving the only home he had ever known.

They started up Hannah's favorite hill. "Pull-Tight," Father called it. At a little level on the side they stopped to let the horses rest.

"Now, if you look yonder through that gap in the trees, Hannah," said Father glancing back over his shoulder, "you can get one last glimpse of the town. For some reason, Mother didn't turn around, and Jonathan was too busy playing.

But Hannah looked, and there it was. She could even see the chimney of their cabin. And there in the distance was the fort with a crimson banner overhead. She had seen Col. Proctor and his First Battalion of men march in with it the day before. And she had seen the picture of a snake with thirteen rattles on it, standing for the number of colonies rebelling against England.

Hannah looked at the flag. She knew that it said, "Don't Tread on Me." Remembering the rattlesnake that almost

killed her mother, she shuddered. A hundred memories
crowded in upon her.

All of a sudden she cried out, "Oh, we forgot my
thimble!"

But it was too late to go back, she knew without being
told. Hannah was a big girl now, and once more choked
back the lump in her throat.

"Goodbye, town," she thought as Father clucked to the
horses to start. "Even if I never see you again, I'll always
feel that you're really my very own."

# *epilogue - rise, thimbler, rise*

SPRING HAD COME TO Hanna's Town once again. A shiny, yellow school bus rumbled down the paved road where pack horses and conestoga wagons used to go. It was loaded with wiggling, giggling children. They passed split rail fences with blue chicory flowers growing around the posts. They rode by clumps of maple trees and plowed fields ready for planting.

As they approached a large white barn on the right, the children in front could read the words, "Hanna's Town Courthouse Farm," painted on the building in big, bold letters. The driver pulled off at the side of the road and parked his bus. The brakes made a loud hissing noise. As the door opened, thirty boys and girls jumped down.

"Now children, stay together and don't run off,"said Mrs. Hayes. The fourth grade teacher gathered the children around her. The group looked curiously at the stakes in the ground, marking places to be dug out. People at various locations were digging between the stakes and searching for buried objects. A guide from the site came over to greet them.

"Let's go over to the museum first," she suggested. "Then we'll return in a few minutes and I'll tell you some of the history of old Hanna's Town."

Mrs. Hayes led the frolicking, noisy children and followed the guide over to a small, stone building.

"Hannah from Hanna's Town, Hannah from Hanna's Town," mimicked a boy in a sing-song voice.

"Timmy, stop teasing Hannah," Mrs. Hayes ordered. "Just because she happens to have the same name as the town that was once here, you don't have to harass her."

The little girl, with hands on hips, promptly turned and made a face at the boy named Timmy.

"Now everyone get a partner and stay in line," the teacher said.

The children lined up and went into the museum. The only noise that broke the stillness of the site now was a huge jet airplane, shooting out from behind a white cloud and into the bright blue sky.

Shortly the children started to come back outside.

"Look," cried one of the boys pointing his finger in the air. They all cupped their hands over their eyes to look up. A long vapor trail was visible across the sky.

"Come along children," urged Mrs. Hayes. "We want to hear all about Hanna's Town now."

The teacher motioned for the children to gather around the guide. She had led them to a spot where one archeologist was digging at the foot of a hillside.

"Shhh, Hush. Timmy, leave Hannah alone," said Mrs. Hayes in a stern voice.

When the children were at last quiet, the guide began:

"Many years ago a little village called Hanna's Town stood on the very ground that you are standing on now."

Some of the children looked down at their feet as if they expected to see traces of the pioneer town.

"An Irishman by the name of Robert Hanna moved here, bought land, and built a log house," the guide went on. "It became such a popular place for travelers between Pittsburgh and Fort Ligonier, that he turned it into an inn."

As the guide told the children the story, they watched the man working a few feet from them. He had measured an area five feet square and was scraping the dirt carefully with a trowel. Every bone and man-made bit of material that he found he placed inside a paper bag marked with the depth in inches, the date, and location. Fragments of blue and white porcelain, pieces of redware pottery, an axe head, a musket ball, an Indian bead, an arrow point, a pewter spoon handle, the stem of a clay pipe, a button of bone, and even straight pins, were already in his bag.

All the dirt that he scraped up he put into a framed wire screen on top of a wheel barrow. The children watched him sift the dirt. Each bucketful brought forth a few more artifacts.

The guide went on with her story.

"The little hamlet grew until it had about thirty houses, a jail, a blacksmith shop, and several inns, one of which was Robert Hanna's courthouse tavern," she said. "It was the first county seat and first place where English courts were held west of the Allegheny Mountains. Just at the beginning of the Revolutionary War the people met here and adopted resolutions that have sometimes been called the Hanna's Town Declaration or Resolves.

"When Indian troubles arose, they built a stockaded

fort. And when a large force of British and Indians attacked the district on July 13, 1782, everyone fled there for safety."

"Were they all killed?" a boy's voice piped up.

"No. Only one girl, who was shot while rescuing a little tot which was about to wander out the gate of the stockade. The child was saved but the girl died shortly after."

"Tell us more," said a girl after a brief silence.

"The raiders burned the whole town, except for the fort and perhaps a house or two."

"What happened to Hanna's Town after that?" asked another.

"The village never recovered from its burning," said the guide. "Another road was built that by-passed it, and most of the people moved away. A new town, called Greensburg, became the county seat and still is today. Even the name, Hannastown, was taken over by a mine village nearby, a hundred years later.

"Old Hanna's Town is only a memory now, and the site has been farm land ever since, until the restoration began recently."

All of a sudden the man digging in the pit felt his trowel strike metal. He could see that it was something more than just a bit of a rusted nail. There it lay in a reddish, burnt area of the ground. Bits of chinking and ashes were buried with it.

The children clustered around and peered down into the pit. Very carefully the man worked his trowel around the piece of metal imbedded in the dirt. It barely showed above the ground. As he unearthed it, the little girl named Hannah cried out: "That looks like a thimble."

The young man picked it up and held it in the palm of his hand. Sure enough, it was what she had thought.

"Whoever owned this could be two hundred years old now, if she were still living," he said. He took a cloth and gently wiped away some of the dirt. As he rubbed, some words began to appear around the rim. Looking at it more closely the young man read out loud, "Forget-Me-Not."

"I wonder who it was that didn't want to be forgotten," he mused. The children were quiet now. They took turns looking at the discovery.

Now the time had come for them to return to the bus. Mrs. Hayes turned to the guide and archeologist, and thanked them. A chorus of children's voices chimed in with their thanks, too. The girls and boys boarded the bus and began to wave and shout as the driver started the motor.

"Hannah from Hanna's Town, Hannah from Hanna's Town," chanted a boy's voice above all the others. The bus pulled out onto the road.

After it disappeared from view, the rolling countryside once more became peaceful and quiet. The stillness of the sky was only broken by the song of an occasional meadow lark in the field.

Now the young man rose up to stretch his legs. He looked at the guide. He was still holding his discovery. "It's just a brass thimble," he repeated.

Only a tiny brass thimble that he held in the palm of his hand. How many years it had been buried deep in the earth, he could not be certain. But one thing he was sure of: "Someone living here loved this thimble. Perhaps it belonged to a woman. Or for all we know, it may even have belonged to some little girl, who lived in Hanna's Town many years ago."